The Secret of Blackbird Cabin

A Cozy Novel by D. L. Tank

PLANERT CREEK PRESS

www.planertcreekpress.com

The Secret of Blackbird Cabin
by D. L. Tank

PLANERT CREEK PRESS
Rhinelander, WI 54501
www.planertcreekpress.com

This is a work of fiction. Unless otherwise indicated, all the names, characters, businesses, places, events and incidents in this book are either the product of the author's imagination or used in a fictitious manner. Any resemblance to actual persons, living or dead, or actual events is purely coincidental.

ISBN (print): 979-8-9867305-3-0
ISBN (ebook): 979-8-9867305-4-7

Printed and bound in the United States of America   1 2

Hope is like a river
that keeps you moving on,
pulls you through the troubled waters,
helps you reach the calm.

Chapter 1

"Tony, check this out," said Megan, pointing to a small, handwritten notice posted in the entryway of the Northwoods Market. "This might be the fixer-upper we've dreamed about."

Tony handed her the rotisserie chicken and set down the bag of groceries so he could put on his reading glasses.

"The price is crazy low," he said. "What do you suppose is wrong with it?"

"Hard to say. Too bad there isn't a picture ... or an address," said Megan, comparing it to the other ads posted for lake homes and cabins. "It'd be fun to at least drive past it."

"Can we look it up online?"

"Nope. There's no realtor listed."

"Weird," said Tony, putting his glasses back in his pocket. "Well, I s'pose we should head back to the cottage before the chicken gets cold."

Fifteen minutes later the couple pulled up to the cabin they were renting for the week in the heart of Wisconsin's Northwoods. Like many Northwoods visitors, they'd often talked about having a place of their own on a lake when they retired.

Retirement had happened two years ago.

But most of the lake homes were out of their price range, and the last thing they wanted to do at this stage of their life was start paying on a mortgage again.

As they were recycling the deli containers from their supper, Megan asked, "Do you think we should call about that cabin? It really would be nice to have a little place of our own, with our own dishes, our own bed."

"And our own favorite chairs," Tony added, lowering his body onto one of the hard, wooden rocking chairs provided with the cottage.

They looked at each other knowingly and smiled.

"Meet you in the car."

A few minutes later, they were back at Northwoods Market, studying the handwritten ad posted outside.

"Hard to imagine it'll last long at this price," said Tony. "Someone else has probably already snapped it up."

"One way to find out," said his wife. She reached over his shoulder and snatched the sign off the wall. "Let's give them a call."

Chapter 2

"This can't be right," Tony grumbled as they slowly made their way down the one-lane, forest service road. "We must have made a wrong turn."

"No," said Megan, studying the notes she'd jotted down while talking to the man on the phone. "He said to head south on the county road... "

"Check."

"Go for about ten miles..."

"Check."

"Then watch for the sign for Sawmill Road on our right."

"Yup. That is where we turned."

They continued down the narrow gravel road through the forest.

"Pretty remote back here," he said. "Nothing but trees."

"I know. It's beautiful, isn't it. So peaceful."

They wove their way through the woods for about five miles without meeting another vehicle, which was a good thing since there weren't many spots wide enough for two cars to pass by each other without scraping against the nearby branches.

For the most part, the terrain was fairly level and the

gravel well packed, but every so often there were dips and Tony had to dodge mud-lined potholes.

"There aren't any buildings back here," said Tony after another five minutes. "We must have taken the wrong road."

"Did you see that!?" Megan suddenly exclaimed, pointing into the trees.

"See what?"

"A Pileated woodpecker."

"Missed it. I need to keep my eyes on the road."

A minute or two later she spotted something else.

"I think I see a sign up ahead. When we get to it, slow down."

"Slower than this?" he chuckled. "I don't think I've hit twenty since we got in here."

Tony stopped when they reached the sign. It indicated a parking area for a snowmobile trail. At this time of year, it was growing over with weeds.

"We're on the right road," smiled Megan. "The guy said that about a mile after this trail head, we'll come to a small driveway on our left with a rope across it. He said to unhook the rope and drive in."

The driveway was easy to find. Strung onto the rope were several milk jugs that looked like they'd recently been spray painted bright orange.

Tony got out, unhooked the rope and dragged it off to the side.

"We're supposed to come to the cabin in about a mile," said Megan. "That's all I've got."

The driveway was hillier, narrower and had tighter turns than the forest service road. Top speed was ten.

They could see by the bent grass and broken stems that another vehicle had recently bounced it's way down the weed-covered drive ahead of them.

"This is like a slow-motion roller coaster," laughed Megan. "Good thing we don't suffer from motion sickness."

"There's always a first time," said Tony, clutching the steering wheel. "Glad that we have all-wheel drive."

"Stop!"

Tony hit the brakes. "What?!"

Megan stepped out of the car and pointed to a turtle that was hidden in the wheel ruts. She carefully picked it up and moved it off the path in the direction it was headed.

"Good save!" said Tony, high-fiving his wife as she got back into the car. "It blended in with the grass so well, I didn't even see it."

After one last turn, they emerged from the forest into a lovely clearing.

The driveway skirted the cleared area, separating the woods from the meadow. A number of young popple trees and half-grown balsams were randomly intermixed with the woodland phlox, trout lily and springbeauties. Along the edges, the woods were filled with trilliums.

At the end of the driveway was an old, but fairly large cabin, constructed with tall, vertically stacked logs. It appeared to have been painted red at some point, but most of the color had peeled away, leaving the exposed cedar poles. About a hundred yards to the left of the house was a barn with a lean along one side.

They pulled up in front of the cabin. No other vehicle was visible.

Beyond the cabin was the lake, rimmed with mature birch, balsam and maple trees. A Great Blue Heron, surprised to see visitors, took off from a patch of water lilies near the shore.

"Looks like we're the first ones here," said Tony.

"The guy said if we got here before him, we should feel free to look around."

Megan stepped out of the car, breathed in the fresh, pine-scented air and scanned her surroundings. "This place is gorgeous. What's the catch?"

"Looks like no one's lived here for a long time," observed Tony.

"I wonder what happened?" said Megan.

"The owners probably went to town, forgot to leave a trail of bread crumbs and couldn't find their way back. This is about as out-of-the-way as you could get."

"But it's really not. We're only about fifteen miles from town." She looked at her phone. "There's even service out here. Four bars."

They walked up to the cabin. The door was secured with a rusty padlock. Megan tried to peek in the window.

"Kinda hard to see what's inside. The windows are pretty dirty."

"The place looks sturdy enough," Tony commented, tapping his knuckles against the still-solid cedar posts. "The sills and frames look to be in good shape, too."

Together they walked around the back side of the building, toward the lake.

The tranquil chorus of birds singing in the trees and insects buzzing around the wildflowers was suddenly overlaid with the sound of a vehicle in the distance. It seemed to be coming toward them.

A minute later, an older Ford pick-up with a camper emerged from the dense woods.

Chapter 3

"Hi," said the slightly balding driver as he exited the pick-up. He was wearing a pair of khaki Docker's and a short-sleeve, button-down Hawaiian shirt that might have been new thirty years ago.

"Glad to see you found the place," he said as he closed the rusting door to his truck, giving it an extra push with his hip to get it to latch. "I had a bit of a challenge finding it myself when I drove in here this morning. I'd only posted the notice a couple of hours before you called."

He held out his hand to greet the prospective buyers.

"Fred Jackson," he said. "Friends just call me Jackson."

"I'm Tony. This is my wife, Megan."

"Great place, isn't it," said Jackson.

"We've only been here a couple minutes," said Megan, "but from what we've seen, it looks like a lovely spot. Why are you selling it?"

Jackson seemed caught off guard by the question.

"Ah, I'm representing a party from Chicago," he said. "A family, actually. The owner recently died and I offered to sell it for them to settle the estate."

"It doesn't look like anyone has been here for quite some time," said Tony.

"What can you tell us about the place?" asked Megan.

"Not much, I'm afraid. As I mentioned, I just arrived this morning. Besides locating it and stringing up the milk jugs, I've barely set foot on the property."

"The orange jugs helped," said Megan.

"Thanks. I hated to dump out three perfectly good jugs of washer fluid, but I thought I'd need some way to mark the driveway. Based on the county plat map, the property extends from the beginning of the driveway, where the jugs are, to just beyond the far shoreline. It's a small lake, but it could be all yours."

"What can you tell us about the cabin?" asked Megan. "It doesn't look very lived in."

"We can find that out together," Jackson said.

He opened the back of his camper and pulled out a brand-new bolt cutter.

"None of the keys I tried worked."

He cut open the padlock, turned the door handle and gave it a push. The painted wooden door hesitated for a moment, then swung in.

Surprisingly, the cabin was bright and almost cheerful. The windows, none of which had the curtains closed, were covered with dust and spiderwebs, but let in plenty of light. The room was a combination living room, dining area and kitchen.

"I believe the HGTV home designers would call this 'early open concept,'" laughed Megan. "It's bigger in here than it looks from the outside."

The walls were varnished knotty pine. Huge log beams spanned the room from one wall to the other.

There was a table with four chairs near the kitchen

area. An old couch was positioned in front of a field-stone fireplace that was topped with a raw-edged wooden mantel. Sitting on top of the mantel were two very dusty taxidermied ducks and a blackbird. Hanging above the fireplace was a pair of gigantic antlers. A nearby built-in wood box held a small pile of logs.

In the far corner of the room, near a hallway, stood an old Victrola record player.

Megan couldn't resist going over to it and opening the lid. There was still an old 78 rpm disk on the turntable.

"Do you suppose it works? The song is 'Bye, Bye, Blackbird.'"

Jackson smiled. "Make this place your own and you can find out."

"I don't see any outlets or light switches," said Tony. "Doesn't look like it has electrical service."

"Electric service would be a pain way out here," said Jackson "Every time there's a storm, your power'd go out."

He stepped over to the window and scanned the bright, sun-filled meadow.

"This would be a perfect spot for solar panels," he said. "No wires to go down. And no electric bills!"

"That might be a possibility," said Tony to Megan. "The price of solar has really come down. And from what I've read, it's not that hard to install if you aren't tying it into the power grid."

Down the hall were two bedrooms, each of which had two windows and a decent-sized closet. The room on the left, which faced the meadow, had two log bunk beds with metal springs and nearly flat mattresses.

The other bedroom looked out at the lake. Against the far wall was a full-sized bed with an ornate wooden headboard and a large, matching dresser. Flanking the bed were two log night stands, each with an oil lamp.

"There's a new refinishing project for you," Tony said to his wife.

Megan ran her hand over the dusty wood. Carved into the headboard was the figure of a bird sitting on a branch, surrounded by leaves.

"I think it's solid oak. With a little work, this could be beautiful. I'd love to have seen this place when it was new."

"It looks like it was well built," said Tony, inspecting the framing around the windows. "It's not just an old hunting cabin. Someone put some effort into building it. It has potential."

Megan stepped out of the bedroom and opened the third door in the hallway.

"I found the bathroom," she announced. "There's a wash stand and a china basin in here and a mirrored medicine cabinet built into the wall. No toilet. But there is a chair with a toilet seat and a covered bucket under it."

"Plenty of room for a composting toilet," enthused Jackson, looking in behind Megan. "It's on an outside wall, so that would work nicely for clean out."

"I did notice an outhouse in the back," said Megan. "Glad to see that isn't the only option."

The group walked back into the kitchen area.

"Look at this," Megan said, focusing on the fancy Monarch wood stove. "It's still in perfect shape."

Tony joined her, twisted the damper control a couple

of times and gave the stovepipe a shake. "Seems solid enough."

Megan looked over the rest of the kitchen area.

"There's no faucets in the kitchen sink," she noted. "Just a hand pump on the sideboard."

"Which means there's an indoor source of water!" beamed Jackson. "No tramping down to the lake with a bucket!"

Tony gave Jackson a look that made it clear he'd about reached his limit of overly positive comments.

"Just trying to look on the bright side," said Jackson, shrugging his shoulders. "You have to expect to do some upgrading at this price."

"Which raises a question," said Megan. "Why is the price so low?"

"As you can see, it'll take some work."

He hesitated a moment.

"And there's something else. I was told that a number of years ago a body was discovered here, under the barn. A hunter's dog found it. Not the sort of thing that attracts buyers."

"That's horrible," said Megan. "Who was it?"

"No one knows. The body was never identified. The authorities figured the person had been dead for a long, long time."

Jackson paused for a moment, as if he was trying to visualize the scene. "I can imagine the body dressed in clothes from the 1930s. There was no ID and back when the body was found, the police didn't have access to a data base of missing persons who fit the description."

"Maybe he was lost and went into the barn to get out of

a storm or something," offered Megan.

"Or," Tony said, stepping into his wanna-be mystery writer persona, "maybe he was a gangster, hiding from the G-men."

"You read too many old whodunits," laughed Megan.

"Not possible," smiled her husband.

Jackson quickly jumped into the conversation.

"According to what I heard, there was no indication of foul play, but no one from the family stayed up here after that. It's been vacant ever since."

"Why's it for sale now?" asked Megan.

"As I mentioned, the owner died recently. His heirs asked me to sell it to settle the estate."

Megan and Tony spent the next forty-five minutes exploring the property, walking the lake shore and checking out the cabin more closely.

Jackson followed them around like a lost kitten looking for a home, putting a positive spin on anything and everything that he thought might raise a red flag for his potential buyers.

Chapter 4

"Did Fred Jackson strike you as kinda weird?" Tony asked as they drove back to the cottage.

"Definitely an odd duck."

"Seemed kinda pushy. Determined to unload the place. But, then, I guess his job is to sell the place."

"Maybe that could work to our benefit," considered Megan. "Did it seem like a place that would work for us? I rather liked it."

"It's different than any of the other places we've looked at," Tony answered. "It certainly is beautiful back there."

"And very private."

"Needs some work, but not as much as you'd expect for that price."

"It's close enough to town that it'll be an easy run for building supplies when we're fixing it up."

When they got back to the cottage, Megan pulled out a note pad and a pen.

"Let's make a list of pros and cons."

"Good idea. One pro would be ..."

"Wait," she said. "We need to give it a name. The fixer-upper programs always give the homes cute names to help buyers decide which one to purchase."

"How about the Waaaaaay Back Cottage."

"Sounds like a portal for time travel."

"Which could be fun."

"But not what we're looking for."

She thought for a moment. "How about Blackbird Manor? There was that blackbird on the fireplace mantel. And another one carved onto the headboard."

"Hmmmm. Not bad. Wasn't the song on the Victrola about a blackbird?"

"That's right. It was 'Bye Bye Blackbird.'"

"Blackbird Manor... Blackbird Manor... " He rolled it around in his brain. "Too pretentious. How about Blackbird Cabin?"

"Perfect!" said Megan, writing it across the top of the note pad."

Throughout the evening they filled in the pros and cons of the place.

The pros side was longer than the cons.

They loved the setting and could easily imagine themselves sitting outside, watching the heron catch fish along the lake shore.

The bones of the house seemed solid enough so that remodeling shouldn't be a massive undertaking. There was plenty of room for solar panels to be placed on the south side of the building.

The more they talked, the more excited they got about the challenge of renovating it. It would be the perfect project to keep them energized in their retirement.

Megan wondered if it was wise to pull money out of their IRA so that they could pay in cash.

"It's a *retirement* account," Tony pointed out. "We're retired. This is why we put money into it."

Together they scanned their list.

Something seemed to be missing.

"What about the body?" said Tony. "Does that freak you out, to know that someone was found dead there?"

"A little. But it was so long ago."

"Yeah, his ghost has probably passed into the light by now."

Megan wrote at the bottom of the page: Dead guy: neither pro nor con.

She scanned the lists, then circled the word 'Pros' at the top.

"The Pro side wins," she announced. "Should we make an offer?"

"Sounds like a plan."

First thing the next morning, Megan called Fred Jackson. She put the phone on speaker.

After a half dozen rings, he answered.

"Hello."

He sounded like he just woke up.

"Hi," said Megan. "We've been talking about the cabin and were hoping to meet with you. We could come to your office today."

"Okay. Sure," he mumbled. "How about I meet you at the Family Restaurant on the edge of town? In about an hour?"

She looked to Tony for confirmation. He nodded.

"That should work. See you then."

"Jackson never told us where he was from, did he?"

Tony said after they hung up. "He didn't even give us a business card."

"Maybe he's a personal friend of the family from Chicago. He said he was helping the owner settle an estate."

Tony checked online to see what would be involved to withdraw some of their retirement savings. Turns out it would be as simple as clicking a few keys, waiting three days for the money to be transferred to their personal account, and then asking the credit union to issue a cashier's check.

Thirty years of putting money into the account, he thought, *and three minutes to take it out.*

An hour later they pulled into the Family Restaurant parking lot. Jackson's old pick-up camper was already there.

They found him inside, at a corner booth in the back, finishing his breakfast.

"Good morning," he said. "Pretty great place, isn't it."

Tony glanced around the restaurant.

"Seems nice enough."

"I mean the cabin."

"Oh, right."

"Super spot back there," Jackson enthused. "You ready to snap it up? I don't think it'll last long."

Geez, this guy is a pain, thought Tony.

"Have you had any other offers?" Megan asked.

"Is the moon made of green cheese?" Jackson joked.

Megan and Tony looked at each other.

Should we run now, while we still can escape?

"I'm just yankin' your chain," laughed Jackson, realizing he was about to lose them. "Seriously, what did you think of the place?"

The couple told him about the property's pros and cons, without sounding too enthusiastic. They didn't want to come across as an easy sell.

"Sounds like it's just the place you've been looking for," said Jackson.

"It is," said Megan, looking at Tony. "I think we're ready to submit an offer for you to take to the seller."

"No need for that," Jackson responded. "I have full authority to make the sale. Are you good for the $75,000 asking price?"

"Well," countered Tony, "since there are quite a few things we'd need to do, we thought $65,000 would be fair."

Silence.

"That would be cash?" Jackson asked.

"A cashier's check, actually."

"That would work. And no contingencies? No building inspection? Everything as is? Whatever's there is yours to deal with?"

Megan nodded.

Jackson sat silent for a moment, then smiled.

He extended his hand.

"Make it seventy grand and it's yours."

Tony and Megan looked at each other, nodded, and they all shook on it.

"What's the next step?" Tony asked. "It's been a long time since we've purchased a home, and that was with a mortgage through a realtor. A title company did all of the paperwork."

"This will be much simpler," said Jackson. "I'll have a quit claim deed drafted and signed, which you'll then take to the register of deeds office at the courthouse. There's a small filing fee and that's it."

"We could get the cashier's check by Friday," said Tony. "Where would you like to meet?"

"This corner table works for me. See you at one on Friday."

Chapter 5

For the next two weeks, Megan and Tony shuttled back and forth from their new cabin in the Northwoods to their home in Eau Claire, where they'd both taught at the university. Tony retired from the English Department two years earlier, Megan from the Chemistry Department the year after that.

"I can't believe it's ours," Megan said as they finally took the time to stretch out in their new, reclining lawn chairs facing the lake.

"Feels good, doesn't it," said Tony. "Seems like it was meant to be."

The place was quickly starting to come together. They'd spent the first week cleaning and hauling away refuse, including old mattresses and a collection of rusty food cans they'd found in the kitchen. Once the windows had been washed, the daylight streamed inside.

The water pump was their first priority. Fortunately, pitcher pumps were available locally and Tony was able to replace it without too much difficulty.

"All primed and ready to go," he glowed as he began pumping cool, clear water into the kitchen sink.

"Ah, Tony," Megan called from the bedroom, "did you

check the drain? There's water running down the hall."

Tony made a quick trip back to the store for a new drain pipe and trap, while Megan mopped up the floor. Soon, the sink was draining perfectly.

Visits to the hardware store were a daily occurrence.

"Glad that we found a place within easy driving distance to town," said Tony.

The item they were most excited about installing was the DIY solar panels. The kit came with roof clips, so Tony decided to mount the solar panels on the south-facing roof. The biggest challenge was convincing Megan that he wouldn't fall off while installing them. The additional purchase of a safety harness and a nylon rope to tie around the chimney sealed the deal.

The roof was in surprisingly good shape. Someone had done a good job of building the place.

Tony finished mounting the roof panels, the sat down with Megan to take a break.

"I plan to install the inverter tomorrow," he told her. "If I put everything together correctly, by tomorrow night we should be able to plug in a couple of lamps. Maybe even run the microwave. I'll still need to run wires to the individual rooms, but it's a good start."

"That's my guy," she said with a smile.

Tony took a seated stage bow.

"I've got an idea," said Megan. "How about we celebrate our last night without electricity with a candlelight supper. I think we deserve it."

"Good idea," he answered. "I could pick up a bucket of ribs and a couple of those good buns from the deli."

"Don't forget to grab a bottle of cranberry wine from

the winery."

While Tony went out to get the food and wine and a few more electrical supplies, Megan prepared the room for their soiree. She set the table with assorted plates, glasses and utensils left by the previous owners. With a couple of new candles in the centerpiece, it looked quite elegant, in a rustic sort of way.

Still needs something, she thought.

A few minutes later she was wandering through the meadow picking a bouquet of wildflowers. An old bottle that she'd come across in a cubby above the wood box made a perfect vase.

By the time Tony returned, the main room of the cabin had been transformed from a tool-strewn workspace into a warm and cozy retreat.

"We need some music," said Tony. "Have you tried that old Victrola?"

"I cleaned it, but didn't try to play it. I was worried I might break something."

She stepped over to the antique record player and raised the lid. The old 78 record was still on the platter, right where she'd noticed it when they'd first looked at the cabin.

She gently lifted the disc to read the label.

"This was recorded in 1926 by Sam Lanin's Dance Orchestra."

"Ah, yes. Sam Lanin," joked Tony. "Always one of my favorites."

"That's 'cause you probably remember him from when you were a teenager."

"Very funny. I'm only a year older than you, so be

careful what you imply."

"This is a really interesting label. There's an image that looks like a devil playing a horn."

Tony came over and took a closer look.

"I think that's supposed to be Pan playing his pipe. Kinda creepy."

"I think it's cool. We should frame it and hang it beneath a 'Welcome to Blackbird Cabin' sign."

"Are you going to make the sign?"

"I'll do that if you frame the record."

"Deal. But let's listen to it first."

Megan carefully set the record back onto the green felt-covered platter and gently placed the needle on the disc.

Nothing happened. She lifted the needle back off the platter.

"I don't think it works."

Tony studied the machine for a minute, then slowly and gently cranked the handle on the side. At first, it turned so easily he wondered if the crank was no longer attached to anything inside, but after several revolutions he could feel the resistance increasing. He cranked it a few more turns and nodded to Megan.

She placed the needle back on the edge of the record. Nothing.

Disappointed, she lifted the needle and moved the arm back to its resting position. Then she noticed a shiny chrome lever next to the platter and gave it a push. The record began to spin, just a little at first, haltingly, then a bit faster.

Tony smiled and gave it a few more cranks. The turntable settled into a uniform rotation.

"Wow, that thing spins really fast," said Megan. "Here goes."

She gently moved the arm over the spinning shellac disc and lowered the needle.

For a few seconds, the only sound was a rhythmic tick, tick, tick.

Then, all of a sudden, someone began singing.

The voice was scratchy, but the lyrics were easy to understand:

> *Pack up all my cares and woe,*
> *Here I go, winging low*
> *Bye, bye, blackbird*
> *Where somebody waits for me*
> *Sugar's sweet, so is she*
> *Bye, bye, blackbird*
> *No one here can love or understand me*
> *Oh, what hard luck stories they all hand me*
> *Make my bed and light the light,*
> *I'll arrive late tonight*
> *Blackbird, bye, bye*

When the record finished playing, she flipped it over. Unfortunately, there were several deep scratches on the other side.

"This side looks unplayable," she said. "Maybe there are some more records inside the cabinet."

The door at the bottom of the record player was stuck. Tony grabbed a table knife to pry it open.

There was nothing in the cabinet except a small tin container with extra needles and the sleeve for the record they'd just played.

Megan pulled out the sleeve. Inside was a folded piece

of paper.

"Look at this. Someone wrote down the lyrics to the song."

> *Pack up all your cares and go,*
> *There you go, winging low*
> *Bye, bye, blackbird*
> *There some booty waits for you*
> *Sugar's sweet, start anew*
> *Bye, bye, blackbird*
> *No one here can love or understand you*
> *Oh, what hard luck stories they will hand you*
> *Check my bed and light the light,*
> *I'll arrive late some night*
> *Blackbird, bye, bye*

"These don't seem right," said Megan, studying the handwritten lyrics. "Whoever wrote this wasn't much of a speller, either. They spelled 'somebody' wrong."

She gave the player a couple of cranks, flipped the lever and placed the needle back on the record.

Megan held the lyric sheet between them so they could compare the words as they listened.

"Definitely got some of them wrong," laughed Tony. "Reminds me of when I was a kid and we were all trying to figure out the lyrics to 'Louie, Louie.' Everybody heard something else. And there were all kinds of ideas what the words meant."

"Didn't that song have hidden clues or something?"

"You're thinking of the Beatles' songs with clues that Paul McCartney was dead." He laughed, recalling to himself his attempts at solving that mystery long ago. "Maybe we should play the record backwards."

Megan gave him a hug. "How about we just let it be. We've got a another busy day tomorrow."

Chapter 6

The following morning, Tony finished connecting the solar panels. It was clear and sunny and he was able to test it out immediately. Everything worked fine.

He ran a wire in through the kitchen window to get things started. Extending lines to the other rooms could wait for another day, when it was rainy and they couldn't work outdoors.

The next big project to tackle would be the installation of the composting toilet. The outhouse had been serving them well, but trekking outside in the middle of the night was getting a bit old.

The plumbing supply store had notified them that the toilet components were in, so after lunch—which was calzones heated up in their newly connected micro-wave—they hooked up the trailer and headed into town.

They'd ordered the high-end waterless toilet that had a tank under the floor that would only need to be cleaned out once a season from the outside.

Tony had been eager to cut the holes in the floor and wall even before the composting toilet arrived, but Megan convinced him to wait, so he'd know precisely where to make the cuts.

Now that he had the components in front of him, he was ready to begin the installation.

A quick perusal of the now-empty bathroom told him that the stool would fit nicely against the outside wall with minimal work. As he measured the dimensions of the small space, however, something seemed a bit off. Based on where the adjoining kitchen wall was located, it seemed like the bathroom should be wider.

Above the spot where the wash basin sat, which was against the opposite side of the kitchen wall, was the medicine cabinet with the mirror. He figured that whoever built the bathroom wall, must have left space between it and the kitchen wall to accommodate the built-in cabinet.

He removed four screws, pulled the cabinet out of the wall and peered into the hole. The space was larger than expected, at least a foot deep. Behind it he could make out the framing for the kitchen wall.

"Megan," he called. "Come in here and look what I've found. Bring a flashlight."

"Cool," she said sarcastically as she stepped behind Tony, flashlight in hand. "A hole."

"Not the hole. The space behind the hole. I think we can remove this wall and have enough room to add a shower. The kitchen's on the other side, so once we get an actual pump, we should be able to connect the bathroom supply to the kitchen supply."

"That would be great."

"You want to help me take down a wall?"

"Sure," said Megan. "We haven't had any fun knocking down walls, like they do on TV. I'm up for helping with the demo. Bring on the sledge hammer!"

Megan was disappointed to learn that there would be no smashing through plasterboard with a sledgehammer, like every home remodeling show seemed to feature. The wall was built with pine boards, not drywall, so it had to be pulled apart one board at a time, with a pry bar and claw hammer. They saved each of the boards, which could be reused for framing the wall around the shower.

Once the wall was down, they discovered another framed-out box, larger in size than the medicine cabinet, but with no opening into the bathroom.

"That's odd," said Tony. "I wonder what that's for? Looks like it opens into the kitchen."

"One way to find out."

They walked around the corner and into the kitchen. Against the wall, the back of which they'd just revealed, was a six-foot tall enameled metal cabinet. The top half had a couple of cabinet doors above two drawers. The bottom section, which stuck out farther than the top, had a couple of drawers for utensils and two doors for storage underneath.

Between the top and bottom sections was an enameled work area, backed by a couple of open shelves.

The entire cabinet, which was built as a single unit, sat flush against the wall.

"No opening there," said Megan. "When I cleaned it out, I noticed that all the cupboards are sealed in the back. Totally mouse proof."

Tony scratched his head.

"Let's see what's behind it."

He gave it a tug, but it didn't budge.

"Wow, this thing is heavier than it looks. Most of these old steel cabinets weigh almost nothing."

He shined the flashlight inside the cupboards to see if the back was screwed to the wall, which would make sense so it wouldn't tip forward.

No screws.

He tried sliding it from side to side, but it didn't budge an inch. There was no space for his fingers behind it, so he grabbed onto one of the drawer handles for a better grip.

The drawer simply slid forward.

Okay, he though, *that was dumb*.

Megan did her best to keep her thoughts to herself.

He held the drawer in place with his left hand, then pulled on the handle with his right.

Snap!

"Damn!"

One side of the handle had come lose. It now looked more like a droopy lever than a drawer pull.

He pushed it back into place and felt it snap into position. He gave it a gentle pull and the drawer slid out as it should.

He held the drawer shut again with his left hand and pulled on the handle, this time more gently.

Snap!

Once again, it had become a lever.

He looked at his wife.

She gave a slight nod.

Tony gave the handle a twist and could feel something turning inside the cabinet.

Then, still holding the drawer in place, he pulled on the

handle again.

The right side of the cabinet began to move forward. He gently pulled the cabinet away from the wall as if it were a door on a hinge, which it pretty much was.

Megan watched without saying a word.

As the cabinet opened further, they could see the no-longer-hidden compartment.

Their silence made the situation feel mysterious, maybe even a little sinister. Being at a loss for words was not a common state for either of them.

"Okay, that's pretty weird," Tony finally said, somewhat under his breath.

Megan shone the light into the opening. The only item in the hidey hole was a green, carnival glass canister with an enameled metal top. Painted on the side, in beautiful art deco lettering, was the word SUGAR.

"Weird place to store one's baking supplies," Tony quipped.

"I know that sugar can create cavities," Megan laughed, "but I never imagined it could create one this big. Let's see what we've found."

Tony carefully removed the jar from the cavity and placed it on the table. It was heavier than he expected. Through the opaque glass, they could see that there was something inside, but couldn't tell what.

Tony tried to unscrew the lid, but it was stuck tight.

"You hold the jar and I'll turn the lid," he said.

Megan held it tight while Tony wrenched off the lid with both hands.

Inside the jar they could see a packet of something wrapped in brown paper, tied up with string.

"Cool," said Tony, "we've found Julie Andrew's stash of favorite things."

"With our luck, it'll probably be her collection of whiskers from kittens."

"Maybe it's pirate's booty."

"Oh, right," said Megan. "Booty from all of the pirate ships patrolling the lakes of Northern Wisconsin."

"Hey, we've got our very own coastline right here. Maybe it was a tiny little pirate on a tiny little ship. Think Stuart Little with a peg leg and eye patch."

She shook her head and rolled her eyes.

"Let's see what treasures we've actually found," she said, reaching into the jar. She pulled out the paper-wrapped packet and set it on the table. Beneath it she found a folded brochure filled with numbers.

She opened the brochure first.

It was a timetable for the Chicago and Northwestern Railroad showing when the trains ran from Chicago to the Northwoods.

"I remember seeing those at the Railroad Museum," said Tony. "When's it from?"

Megan looked it over and found a date at the bottom. "It's from 1932."

Tony reached out and picked up the paper-wrapped bundle.

"My turn," he said.

He untied the string from the parcel and removed the brown paper.

Inside was a stack of currency.

"Wow! I was right about the pirates' booty!"

"Oh my!" Megan said. "I need to check something."

She hurried to the Victrola and grabbed the sheet with the hand-written lyrics.

"Listen to this."

*There some **booty** waits for you*
***Sugar's** sweet, start anew*
Bye, bye, blackbird.

"I think the lyrics were left as a clue."

Chapter 7

"A clue to what?" asked Tony.

"I'm not sure. But this seems like more than a coincidence."

Tony started to sort the currency into piles. There were hundred dollar bills, fifties, twenties, tens, and singles. Even a few two-dollar bills. Many of them looked like they'd hardly been used.

Tony thumbed through the bills, doing a quick calculation in his head.

"There's over two thousand dollars here."

"What do you suppose we should do with it? Do we need to report it to someone?"

"Seems to me that it came with the property, same as the furniture. Jackson specifically said that everything came with the place. As far as I'm concerned, it's ours. Think of it as a house warming gift."

Megan picked up the cash and studied it.

"These bills look different than our money does today."

"Is there a date on them?"

She looked closely at one of the bills.

"This one says 'Series of 1928.' I wonder if they're still any good?"

She paused.

"What if they're counterfeit? I don't want to get arrested for passing counterfeit bills."

"Tell you what. When we go into town next, let's take a few of them to the credit union and see what they think. We don't have to say we discovered a whole stash, just that we wondered if they were still usable."

The next day, after picking up a few groceries, they stopped at the credit union with a sampling of the bills. They where informed that the currency was still legal tender.

"Old bills are redeemable for face value," said the cashier, doing a quick calculation. "So these together are worth one hundred and eighty-three dollars. Would you like to deposit them into your account?"

"Not today, thank you," Megan responded. "We were just wondering what they were worth."

The cashier typed a few numbers into her computer.

"If this amount had been invested back in 1928, back when the bills were new, they'd be worth more than three thousand dollars today. We have some great rates on CDs right now. I'd be happy to help you get things started."

The customer at the adjacent cashier's booth seemed to be eavesdropping. He glanced over at the old bills before stepping away from the counter.

Tony and Megan thanked the cashier for the information and headed back to their car.

"Good to know they're still worth something," said Tony to his smiling wife.

"And that they're not counterfeit."

As they were getting into their car, they were stopped by the customer who had overheard them talking with the cashier.

"Excuse me," he said "I don't mean to be rude, but I couldn't help overhearing your conversation about those old bills. I collect and sell old coins and currency and might be able to help you."

He handed them a business card: Northwoods Coin & Collectables. William Kunze, prop.

"Old currency is worth more than face value to collectors," he offered. "Sometimes, a lot more. I'd hate to see you just cash them in and lose out on their true value. If you'd like more info, I'm always willing to chat, no pressure to buy or sell anything."

Tony passed the card over to Megan.

"Thanks," she said, glancing at the card and putting it in her purse. "Nice meeting you."

"That was interesting," Tony said as they pulled out of the parking lot. "Might be worth checking out sometime."

Chapter 8

"You ready to explore the barn this morning?" Tony asked Megan when they'd finished breakfast. "I'm kinda curious about where they found that body. Maybe there's a connection to the hidden cash."

The two of them had been so busy working in and around the cabin that they'd barely peeked inside the other structure. That and the fact that they'd tacitly been avoiding the subject of the body found there.

"Where do you suppose they found the guy?" Megan asked as they pulled open the large wooden door.

"No clue. Maybe there'll be some scraps of police tape or something."

The building didn't actually look much like a barn. There were no stalls, no feed bins, no hay loft. It was just one large room with a wooden plank floor with some burn marks and a chimney running through the middle of the roof.

A bow saw, a few ropes and some pulleys were hanging on the wall and a half dozen gardening tools were propped in one corner. Aside from that, and a good coating of dust and spider webs, the room was empty.

Lining the back wall were a number of built-in shelves

and four, tall built-in cabinets, each with a door that was decorated with a wood-burned image of an animal or bird. A quick scan showed nothing of particular interest on the shelves; old paint cans, a box of chains, miscellaneous plumbing pieces.

Tony had a thought.

"According to Jackson, a hunter's dog found the body, so it must have been found outside. The dog wouldn't have wandered inside here. Maybe under the lean?"

They stepped back outside without looking in the cabinets and walked around to the side of the barn. Several old pieces of unrecognizable machinery and a pile of bent and twisted scrap metal were under the shed roof. There was also an abandoned lawn mower covered with a tattered canvas tarp.

Near the back of the lean they found a metal rowboat flipped upside down. The oars were leaning against the wall behind it.

"Check this out," said Tony.

He raised the edge of the boat. Beneath it was a concave depression.

"Since it was hunting season, maybe the guy got lost in a snow storm, hid here under the boat and died of exposure."

"Why wouldn't he have just gone inside? Besides," Megan pointed out, "Jackson said it was hunting season when they *found* the body. We don't know when he died."

Megan studied the space under the boat.

"This looks more like an animal den, anyway," she said, pointing out the leaves, fur and animal droppings packed inside the burrow. "Too small for a body."

"I've been kinda trying to ignore this whole body thing," admitted Tony. "You too?"

"Yup. Not really something I've wanted to think about."

"It would be interesting, though, to know more about what happened. Maybe we could solve a cold case."

"Well," said Megan, "you've been talking about writing a mystery novel since you retired. Now's your chance to finally get started."

"Yeah. I suppose."

Megan noted his lack of a positive response.

Even though he'd taught writing for years, he had yet to actually create the next best seller. It was a whole lot easier to talk about writing, than to actually do it. Especially something as complicated as a full-length whodunit.

"You enjoy watching shows where the mysteries are ripped from the headlines, right?" Megan asked supportively.

"True."

"So, this is your chance," she laughed. "We have our very own headlines from which you can rip."

Tony thought for a moment, then gave her a smile.

"Nice having you for my muse."

"So, where do we start?"

Tony speculated that the local museum might have old news clippings about the body being found.

"An unsolved murder would be the sort of thing they'd probably have information about."

"Who said it was a murder?"

"Who would read a murder mystery about a dead guy that nobody reported missing who probably died of exposure with no suspicion of foul play and many years later was accidently found behind a barn by a dog? That doesn't sound all that intriguing."

"As the writer, it'll be your job to make it intriguing. I suspect that most of the ripped-from-the-headline stories that we see on TV were not nearly as exciting in real life. Or death."

* * * * *

They pulled into the museum parking lot shortly after lunch. Their plan was to first show someone at the museum the railroad timetable they'd found, and then, if the person seemed eager to talk with them, casually bring up the body.

They were greeted by a woodsy-looking young man with a beard as they walked through the front entrance.

"Welcome to the Northwoods Museum. Have you been here before?"

"We have," said Megan. "We've noticed that you have a nice collection here of railroad artifacts and thought you might be interested in seeing an old timetable that we came across."

She held out the document.

"I'm Kenny, the museum director," the man said, carefully taking the timetable. "Are you from around here?"

"I'm Megan. This is Tony. We bought a small lake cabin last month. We found this hidden in one of the walls."

"It's in really good shape for such an old document," Kenny noted, gently unfolding it and checking both sides. "These were more or less throwaway items, so they were printed on pretty thin paper."

"What can you tell us about it?" Tony asked.

"This is a timetable from the Chicago and Northwestern Railroad showing the scheduled stops for the passenger trains between Chicago and the Northwoods.

"It's from 1932," he continued. "Back then, the trains only ran during the warmer months, primarily to bring tourists up from Illinois. They'd be picked up at the station and taken to the resort where they'd stay, often for a few weeks, sometimes for the whole summer."

"How about folks who had their own cabins?" asked Megan, beginning to shift gears. "Would they take the train, too?"

"By the '30s, many folks had their own cars, so wealthier visitors to the Northwoods could drive up here. But the train was still important. You could usually find someone to pick you up from the station and take you to your lake cabin."

"Speaking of lake cabins," Tony said. "The cabin that we just bought has a bit of a mystery that you might be able to help us with. Do you have another minute?"

"To talk Northwoods history? Always."

"We were told that a man's body had been discovered on our property quite a few years ago, but was never identified," began Tony.

He could see that he had Kenny's attention.

"The body was believed to have been there since the 1930s, but only discovered by a hunter about twenty or thirty years later."

"And you said the body was never identified?"

"Correct," said Tony. "We were hoping you could help us figure that out."

"We thought maybe you'd have old newspaper clippings about the body's discovery," clarified Megan. "Seems like it would have been a big news story."

"Where is your cabin?"

"About fifteen miles south of here, hidden way back in the woods, surrounded by county forest."

The couple could practically see the wheels spinning in the museum director's history-filled brain.

"Right off the bat," he said, "nothing comes to mind. You said the body was discovered several decades ago?"

"Something like that," said Tony. "We don't know an exact date."

"And the person was believed to have died in the 1930s?"

"That's what we were told."

"That would have put it right during the time when bootlegging was a big business up here. And the location would make sense for that, too. But right off hand, I can't think of any specific cases."

"We just thought it'd be worth asking," said Tony. "Thanks for the info about the timetable."

"I appreciate your asking," said Kenny. "Now you've got my curiosity. Anything else I can help you with?"

"We'll just snoop around the museum a bit," said Megan. "We decided to take a day off from working on the cabin. Everyone told us that when you get a lake cabin of your own, you spend most of the time there maintaining it. And so far, they're right."

"Have you checked out the free concerts at Lakeside Park?" offered Kenny. "The band playing this evening is very popular."

"What sort of music do they play?" Tony asked. More than once they'd attended concerts by local musicians only to discover they played all original tunes and nothing they could recognize and relate to.

"They're a variety band specializing in oldies. Stuff by the Eagles, Fleetwood Mac, even a few Beatles tunes."

"That sounds pretty good," said Megan. *I can leave my reading material at home,* she thought.

"Local restaurants bring out their food trucks, too," added Kenny. "It's always a fun way to spend a summer evening on the big lake."

* * * * *

Determined to spend a day without doing any renovations, Tony and Megan filled the afternoon exploring the area's antique shops and thrift stores.

"What do you think?" Tony asked as it neared supper time. "Should we have supper at the park and take in the concert?"

"I'm game for that. It feels good to not be spending the day working."

The gravel lots were already filling with cars when they pulled into Lakeside Park. Folks of all ages were setting up lawn chairs and laying out blankets.

"Looks like we were supposed to bring our own seating," said Tony.

Megan scanned the area in front of the band shell.

"We're fine," she said, pointing to an open picnic table about midway to the stage.

As the band was finishing up its sound check, lines

began to form at the food trucks.

"What would you like?" said Tony. "I'll go get some food and you can hold our seats."

"Surprise me."

A few minutes later he returned with two huge gourmet burgers on hard roll buns and a tray of deep fried cheese curds. Stuck under his arms were a couple bottles of draft root beer and a stack of napkins.

As they dug into their meal, the band opened with a rousing rendition of "Old Time Rock & Roll," followed quickly by "Born to be Wild" and "Rhiannon."

"Good band," said Tony. "I'm glad the museum guy recommended them."

"Speaking of the museum guy, I think he's sitting over there," Megan said, nodding toward a couple and child sitting on a blanket near the stage.

When the set ended, Megan and Tony decided to stretch their legs with a walk along the lake front.

"Well, fancy seeing you here," said a voice from behind them. It was Kenny from the museum. "What do you think of the band? The bass player and I went to high school together."

It's a good thing we liked them, thought Megan. *It'd be kind of awkward to say that his friend's band sucked.*

"They sound great," she said. "It's nice to hear music that we recognize."

"By the way," said Kenny. "I checked with a couple other folks who know about local history, and none of them recall hearing about the unidentified body you said was found near your cabin. A quick scan of the newspaper database didn't show anything, either."

"That's odd," said Tony. "Seems like folks would recall something like that."

"There have been a couple other cases that came to mind," said Kenny. "In the '70s, a man was found buried at an old farm about ten miles from your place, but he was quickly identified.

"And, just last year, a body that had been found by a hunter thirty years ago was finally identified by DNA. He had died of exposure. But that was in a different part of the county and doesn't fit your time line."

"That's very strange," said Megan. "I guess we'll have to keep looking."

"Our guess is that whoever told you the story about the body at your place was probably confused; cobbling together those two actual events into one story."

"Thank you for looking into it," said Tony.

"Glad I could help. Now you can sleep without worrying about a ghost tap, tap, tapping on your window pane in the middle of the night."

When they finished walking along the lake front, someone else was at their picnic table. They decided to head back to Blackbird Cabin.

"So," said Megan as they drove home, "do you think Jackson made the whole thing up just to sell us the place?"

"That wouldn't make any sense. He used the body as the reason for selling it at such a low price. Without that bit of history, he could easily have asked more for the place."

"Which means that he must believe the story that he told us," Megan speculated.

"That's my guess. We could ask him for more details. Or at least find out where he got his information, so we'd have an idea where to look ourselves."

"His number's in my phone. Do you think it's too late to call now?"

"It didn't seem like he exactly has office hours. Might as well give it a try. If nothing else, you could leave a message."

Megan called the number she'd used to contact Fred Jackson several weeks earlier.

"That's odd," she said. "All I get is a message saying 'the number you called is no longer in service.'"

Chapter 9

The next morning, after a late breakfast in their chairs facing the lake, Megan tried calling Fred Jackson again with the same result.

"Enough worrying about dead bodies," said Megan. "How about we begin exploring our property. We've got forty acres and about all we've seen so far is the area right around the cabin.

"When we were walking along the lake shore at the park last night, it occurred to me that we haven't explored our own lake, yet. We could start there."

"I was thinking it'd be fun to put in some hiking trails through the woods," said Tony.

"You're just looking for an excuse to use your new chain saw."

"Gee, do you think? You know me way too well. I could pull out that old boat we found behind the barn and see if it floats."

"That's not quite what I had in mind. How about we try to walk around the lake today? Maybe we can figure out where the creek comes into it."

Once they'd put on their heavy pants, boots and sprayed on some bug repellent, they walked down to the lake.

"Which way should we go?," asked Megan. "Clockwise or counter clockwise?"

"Clockwise is probably best," Tony said, way too seriously. "If we go counter clockwise, we might create a time warp and end up back here before we began."

"Okay," Megan said slowly, deciding not to encourage him by reacting to his comment.

They headed left, the lake on their right.

The first hundred yards was easy going because the yard had been cleared along that part of the lake shore. Just past the barn, the backside of which was built into a hill, the shoreline changed and the trees and brush came right down to the water. In some places, there were long-dead tree trunks poking through the surface.

"Glad that we wore our boots," said Megan as they began bushwhacking through the brush. "This is harder going than I expected."

"Nothing I couldn't fix with my chain saw," her husband smiled.

While it was not easy walking, they had to admit that the area was quite magical. The wet areas along the edge were filled with Marsh-marigolds and wild Calla lilies. The trilliums that were carpeting the woods earlier were done blooming, but some daisies were blooming in the sunnier spots.

"Look at this!" said Megan, bending down and gently lifting the leaves of an unusually-shaped purple and green plant. "I found some Jack-in-the pulpits."

"I don't think I've actually seen one of those before," said Tony. "Pretty cool to have them in our own woods."

Megan carefully raised the top of the pulpit to reveal

Jack inside, ready to preach to his woodland congregation.

Despite the tough terrain, they totally enjoyed their hike, immersing themselves in their new environment. They found several animal trails leading to the water.

Because no one had lived in the cabin for so long, the wildlife was quite unaccustomed to visitors and fled as soon as they'd get a glimpse of movement through the trees. The birds, on the other hand, were singing up a storm, uninhibited by the strangers passing beneath them.

Viewed from across the lake, their cabin looked idyllic; a scene waiting to be painted by Thomas Kincade.

"So this is what we look like to the other critters who live here," said Megan. "We need to remember to keep it up to their standards."

About three-quarters of the way around the lake, they heard water running. They soon came to an old beaver dam. Beyond the dam, was the creek.

"I think we can walk across this," said Tony, studying the dam and noticing that it was overgrown with tag alder. "It looks pretty solid."

"It seems like it's become part of the shoreline," observed Megan. "I wonder if the beaver are still around."

Tony studied their surroundings.

"I don't see any beaver-chewed stumps. My guess is they've been gone for quite a few years. Nice that they left us a way to get across the creek."

They began to carefully cross over the dam, then stopped. The middle section of it felt spongy. Beneath their feet, they could see water running through the interwoven branches, cascading into the waiting creek a foot below.

"That's where the sound of running water is coming from," observed Megan. "Do you think it's safe to continue?"

Tony reached down, grabbed a handful of branches and tugged. After a couple of hard pulls, they came out, releasing a small surge of suddenly muddy water. Fortunately, the dam remained intact.

He stepped across the gap with no problem, then reached his hand out to Megan.

Once on the other side of the creek, they decided to explore along the bank of the gravel-bottomed stream. The water was running clear, but walking was hard going. The intertwined tag alder grew close to the creek, often reaching across it to mingle with the branches on the other side. Even though they were only a hundred yards from the cabin, it felt like they were a million miles from civilization. Finding a path through the brush, however, was more challenging than they'd expected. After a few minutes they decided it was time to head back.

"That was fun," Megan said when they returned to their cabin. She plopped down in her chair. "You totally have my permission to clear a trail around the lake. I can already picture myself walking it early in the morning, listening to the birds, maybe catching a glimpse of some critter getting a drink at the water's edge."

"It's already on my list," said Tony. "But I suppose I should finish installing the toilet, first. The forecast is calling for heavy rain."

* * * * *

Tony grabbed his pry bar and prepared to pull away the boards skirting the bottom of the back of the cabin, so there'd be room for the holding tank beneath the bathroom.

To his surprise, the skirting wasn't attached there and tipped over into his hands. Miscellaneous junk was piled under the building. It was as if the folks who'd lived there simply threw their trash under the cabin, then leaned the skirting back against the wall so it wouldn't show.

Makes sense, he thought. *They didn't have weekly trash pickup back then.*

In the area where he needed to put the holding tank, he began pulling the debris out with his hands.

There were lots of rusted cans and old brown bottles.

Looks like the workers enjoyed their brewskies.

Rather than risk cutting himself, he grabbed a rake and started to pull out more of the trash so that he could install a level pad of paving blocks for the tank.

Among the rusty cans and broken glass was a metallic disc of some sort, about four inches across. At first he thought it was the top of a coffee can, but when he picked it up, he could see that it was actually shaped like a six-pointed star. He was surprised by its weight.

He grabbed the bottle of water he had near him and poured some over the curious find.

The accumulated grime came off easily. No rust. It was some sort of metallic medallion.

Across the top, engraved within a raised decorative ribbon, were the words C. & N. W. POLICE.

In the center was a design or logo surrounded by a raised circle. He couldn't make out what it was.

At the bottom of the artifact, in large brass figures, were the numerals 4 0 2 0.

"Megan," he called. "I think you should take a look at this."

"Looks like some sort of police badge," said Megan.

"I can't imagine a badge would be this big," said Tony, handing it to her. "It looks likes a prop. Something clowns would wear."

"It's really heavy."

She spit on it and wiped away some more of the dirt with her thumb, then read aloud: "C. & N. W. POLICE."

After barely a moment's thought, Tony proclaimed, "Got it! It stands for Clown and Nit Wit Police!"

"What?"

"Remember in 'Dumbo,' they had the clown cops?"

"I think those were clown fire fighters," Megan pointed out. "We've seen C. & N. W. someplace before. Hang on a minute."

She hurried into the house and returned a moment later with the time table.

"Maybe it stands for Chicago and North Western."

"I suppose that could be. But why would a railroad have police?"

"No clue."

"Can you tell what that image is in the middle?"

"Not for sure. We'll need to clean it up better. At least it's not a blackbird."

"Just to be on the safe side," Tony joked, "why don't

you check the lyrics sheet to see if anything there fits with a badge. And look for clown clues, too."

She just shook her head.

"You'd better get back to work. It'll be nice to finally have an indoor toilet so we don't have to run outside in the rain."

The toilet went together easier than Tony expected. Megan put the wash basin back in place and tidied up the room as best as she could, given that one wall was awaiting framing for the shower. That would have to wait until another day.

Chapter 10

"I was able to clean up that badge," said Megan, when Tony finished installing the tank and came inside. "I think it's silver. The numbers at the bottom look like copper. Or maybe brass. We'll need an expert to look at it and tell us what treasure we've found this time."

"How about that guy from the coin and collectibles shop? He might know about badges. We could get his thoughts about the money and the badge at the same time."

"There's still plenty of time this afternoon," offered Megan, "We need to pick up a few things for supper, anyway."

Northwoods Coin & Collectables was in a small strip mall that shared the parking lot with the Family Restaurant.

"Hello, again," said William Kunze as they walked in the door. "Did you decide to take me up on my offer to appraise your old currency?"

"We did," said Megan, scanning the glass counters filled with coins and other curiosities. "Cute shop. We were hoping that you could tell us what these bills might be worth to a collector."

She pulled out the stack of bills, still wrapped in the brown paper. William was surprised to see how many she had.

"Looks like your collection has grown since I saw you at the credit union. Have you been collecting long?"

"We're pretty new at it," said Tony. "Is this something you can help us with?"

"Absolutely. I'd be honored to give you an appraisal. I'll need to look at each bill carefully, determine its condition, check the serial numbers, that sort of thing. Do you have a while?"

"We're not in a rush," said Tony.

"Would it work if we left to do a little shopping and came back in, maybe, an hour?" asked Megan.

"That would be fine. I can get started right away."

"Oh, I almost forgot," said Megan, pulling the badge out of her purse. "Could you also tell us about this?"

"Certainly," he said, setting the badge on a black velvet pad next to the stack of bills. "See you in an hour."

"Do you think we should have gotten a receipt?" Tony asked as they stepped out of the store.

"We're probably okay. Besides, he'd have to go through them one by one to know what to put on the receipt."

As they were about to get into their car, they noticed a familiar vehicle parked in front of the Family Restaurant.

"Isn't that Jackson's camper?" said Tony.

"One way to find out," said Megan.

Jackson was sitting at his favorite corner booth, a cup of coffee in front of him, looking through some papers. He didn't notice them walk in.

"Well, hello there, Mr. Jackson," said Tony, surprising him. "Glad we found you."

"We tried calling, but couldn't get through," added Megan.

"Oh, right," he said, trying to quickly amp up his bravado. "I got a new phone. I like to keep up with the latest technology. What can I help you with? Are you enjoying life at the lake?"

"We are," said Megan. "Lovely spot back there."

"We had a question for you," said Tony. "We've been trying to learn more about that body you said was discovered by a hunter under the barn, but we can't find anyone who knows anything about that event. Mind if we sit?"

Megan and Tony slid into the corner booth, one on each side of him.

"We're really curious to know more about what happened," said Megan. "Can you point us to some news articles about it?"

"Oh. That. Right. I've been thinking about that. To be honest, I've never actually seen any articles about it."

"So you made it up?"

"I didn't exactly make it up. But I may have enhanced it a bit? Over time."

"Which means what?"

"When I was a kid, back in Chicago, I remember overhearing my grandpa and his brothers talking about a body buried at a cabin Up North. They seemed pretty excited about it, laughing, in fact. I remember Grandpa saying 'the last words that liar ever heard were, *You can either tell us your name or tell it to St. Peter. Your choice.*'"

"Your grandpa murdered someone at our cabin?!"

"No, I didn't say that. I don't know who they were talking about. Or what cabin. I was just a kid. That's all I heard. But I imagined all sorts of things.

"Grandpa noticed me listening. He took me aside later and asked what I'd heard. I told him *I didn't hear nuthin'*. He said that was good, cause if I ever told anyone what I didn't hear, I'd get to visit St. Peter, too."

"That's horrible!" said Megan. "Did you tell someone? Call the police?"

"The police?" Jackson laughed. "Grandpa was on the police force."

"So you've kept this secret your whole life? Why tell it now?"

"Grandpa died a couple months ago. He can no longer hurt me. All I wanted to do was to sell that cabin. No one had been up here in years."

"But why the story about a body? How would that help you sell it?"

"When you asked why the price was so low, I panicked. I came up with the body story on the spot to explain the low price. I wanted to sell the place quickly and not have to go through a realtor or a building inspection. I wasn't sure what might be found."

"As far as we can tell," said Megan, "there wasn't anything to find. From what we've found out, there never was a body at the cabin."

"That's good for both of us, then," said Jackson, regaining his swagger. "You got a great price on the place of your dreams, and I no longer have to worry about meeting St. Peter. Everyone wins. Now I'd like to get back to my lunch."

"One more question," said Megan as the couple slid out of the booth. "Your grandfather. What police department was he with?"

"Chicago," said Jackson. "A special division that worked with the railroad."

Chapter 11

After picking up their groceries, they returned to the coin shop.

"Hi," said William as they walked in. "Perfect timing. I just finished looking over your collection."

"Great," said Megan. "And what's the verdict?"

"Interesting choice of words," William laughed. "You might be surprised."

"Okay" said Megan. "Now I'm really curious."

"Give it to us straight, Doc," joked Tony. "We can take it."

"First, the badge."

He held it out for them to look at as he described what he'd learned.

"This is what's called a pie plate badge because of its large size. The image in the center is the seal of the city of Chicago. Their police department switched over to this type of badge in the early 1900s because they were difficult to counterfeit."

"Why would anyone counterfeit a badge?" asked Tony.

"To impersonate an officer and then commit a crime. That was a big problem back then."

"So this is authentic?"

"Absolutely. What makes this one uncommon, is that it was issued only to officers who protected the Chicago and North Western Railroad."

Megan poked her husband in the arms: "See, I told you it wasn't Clowns and Nit Wits,"

"What are we looking at as far as value?" Tony quickly asked William.

"The badge looks like it was recently cleaned with an abrasive cleanser, which has lowered its value some-what."

"Whoops," said Megan.

"That said, I would value it between two and three hundred dollars. There are a lot of collectors of railroad items, so I think this would sell quite easily."

"Would we put it on ebay?" asked Tony.

"That's one option. I'd be happy to try to sell it for you on consignment. I'd need to do a little more research on it, and then I would list it online."

"What else do you hope to find out with your research?"

"Badge numbers were unique to the officer. I may be able to identify who it belonged to. If it was worn by someone known in the police or railroad community, that would raise interest considerably."

"Good to know," said Megan. "What about the stack of bills?"

"First off, let me say this is an excellent collection. During the Great Depression there wasn't a lot of cash left-over to save. Folks needed it to buy food and pay the rent. So finding a collection like this, practically untouched, is quite rare."

"I'm glad that you stopped us in the parking lot the

other day," said Megan.

"I am, too," said William. "There is something about your collection that is especially intriguing."

"Such as?" asked Tony.

"Sequential numbers. A number of your bills are numbered sequentially. That usually only happens when the bills are brand new, right out of the bank."

"Which is a good thing, right?"

"Possibly. It means you could sell them as a set, which would increase their value. But it also raises a question: Were these bills stolen?"

"We're going to hate the answer, aren't we?" said Megan.

"I found a news story from 1932 about a bank robbery in the U.P. There were four robbers. Several days later, three of them were caught fleeing the Northwoods and most of the money was recovered. The fourth robber, however, was never seen again."

"And the rest of the money?"

"It was never seen again, either. Until, I believe, today."

Megan gasped. "Are we in trouble for having stolen property?"

"No," he reassured them. "The statute of limitations ran out many, many years ago on these bills."

"That's a relief," said Megan.

William asked if it would be okay for him to mention their find to others, in case he came across a buyer..

"I guess that would be okay," said Tony. "That'll give us some time to decide what we want to do."

"We really appreciate your help," said Megan, picking up the badge and currency. "What do we owe you for the appraisal?"

"Oh, no charge," William smiled. "I have just one request: I'd love to hear how you ended up with this stash."

Chapter 12

The next day Tony decided to brush out the trail around the lake while Megan worked on the yard near the cabin. They'd stopped at the greenhouse on the way out of town and picked up a number of perennials that they thought might be of less interest to the deer.

In the Northwoods, you either build an eight-foot fence around your plants or risk having them eaten, no matter what the tag says. Deer don't seem to understand that if a plant is listed as deer resistant, they're supposed to leave it alone.

Rabbits weren't a problem. Megan had seen several foxes running across their meadow and attributed that to the minimal rabbit population. That and the fact that they regularly saw hawks. *They're probably hunting mice and voles,* Megan thought as she watched one circling overhead, *but a baby bunny would be a tasty treat.*

Her thoughts were interrupted by Tony when he came in for lunch.

"The yard is looking great," he said.

"Thanks. How's the trail coming? I was kind of monitoring your progress by where I heard the chain saw."

"It's going well. Instead of sticking to the shoreline,

I'm weaving in and out of the woods, using some of the deer trails as my guide. I think that'll make for a more interesting walk."

While they were putting together some sandwiches, Megan's phone rang. She didn't recognize the number, but it was local.

"Hi, this is Dawn Hogan from TV12. Is this the Megan who was at the coin shop yesterday?"

"What is this regarding?" she responded suspiciously.

"I was talking with a friend who runs the coin shop and he mentioned that you may have discovered the long-lost stash believed to be from an old bank robbery. I'm always looking for upbeat stories with a local angle, especially stories that tie in to our Northwoods history, and this would be perfect. Would I be able to interview you and shoot some video of where you found it?"

"Ah, just a second. Let me put you on speaker so my husband can be part of this conversation."

The story ran three nights later, at five, six and ten. They'd picked up a cheap TV and a small, over-the-air antenna so they were able to watch it. They figured it wouldn't hurt to be able to tune in the local news once in a while, anyway. About the only other stations they could get without cable were a couple of shopping channels.

Dawn had reassured them that she wouldn't reveal the exact location of their cabin or give the impression that they had done anything wrong in finding the money.

She'd spent about an hour interviewing them and shot video of them re-enacting how the metal cabinet could be pulled away from the kitchen wall to reveal the hidden compartment.

They'd put the bills, once again wrapped up in the brown paper and string, back inside the sugar canister so they could rediscover them before the camera.

Tony couldn't resist repeating his line about discovering Julie Andrews' stash of favorite things. Megan chose not to reprise her line about kitten's whiskers.

Before Dawn had arrived, Megan and Tony had agreed to make no mention of "Bye, Bye Blackbird."

"We don't need folks thinking we're a couple of conspiracy nut cases living in the backwoods," Tony had said to his wife.

"Which we aren't," she'd responded. "Right?"

"Right," he laughed, giving her a hug. "Or, if we are, at least we're each others' nut cases and no one else needs to know about it."

In addition to the interview with Tony and Megan, the story included a historic picture of the bank that was robbed and an interview with the owner of the coin shop.

William emphasized that there was nothing illegal about having the money after so many years. He also said that he'd been able to track down the serial numbers from some of the bills and was confident that they were, in fact, part of the loot stolen from the bank.

"That's good to know," said Megan as they watched the story. "I wish he'd called us, though, instead of our finding that out on TV."

No mention was made of the badge. Dawn had said when she interviewed them, that since the badge was found in a different location and there was no known connection to the cash, she wouldn't include it.

"This is a feel-good story about recovering the stolen money," she'd said to them. "I don't want to turn it into a scandal linking the Chicago police."

"Well," said Megan after the clip ended. "I think that went okay."

"Yes," said her husband. "Better than I expected."

"It's been a good week, hasn't it?" Megan said as they crawled into bed. "I'm glad we learned that the mysterious dead body never really existed."

"Agreed," said Tony. "Kind of funny that it was just a kid's over-active imagination."

"And the money. Now we can stop wondering what to do about it. It's ours, free and clear."

"Don't forget finally getting the toilet installed before it rains. I think that's kind of a big accomplishment."

"Good night," she said, giving her husband a gentle elbow in the ribs. "See you in the morning."

The deluge began about midnight.

Chapter 13

"Sure glad that you finished the toilet," Megan commented the next morning. "Not having to run outside in this storm is quite the luxury."

"Funny how the definition of *luxury* changes depending on one's perspective, isn't it."

"So true. A month ago I wouldn't have imagined that a microwave and a mini-fridge would feel like having a chef's kitchen."

"So, what have you got planned for the day?" Tony asked. "It's too wet to work in the garden."

"No kidding. The plants I put in yesterday, though, should be enjoying the soaking. I was thinking it'd be a good day to start refinishing the headboard. If you'd be willing to help me take it apart and carry it to the barn, I could work on it out there."

"Sounds like a plan. It'll be a good day for me to run the wires to the bathroom and bedrooms."

"That'll be nice. The oil lamps have come in handy, but I'm not a big fan of their smell."

"You know that lamp on my side of the bed," Tony said, "the one we haven't been able to use because it doesn't have a wick? I can get a kit to electrify it. If I do that, though, it can't be turned back into an oil lamp."

"I'd say go for it, as long as we keep a couple of oil lamps for emergencies. And probably for days like this when the solar panels aren't getting any sun."

"Supposedly they'll generate electricity even when it's raining. I'm curious to see if that's true."

"Well, I guess we'll find out."

Tony helped Megan remove the headboard from the bed.

"This is a beautiful piece," Megan said, running her hands over the smooth wood and intricately carved bird and branches. "I wonder if it was built just for this cabin."

"Seems like a good possibility. It fits right in."

When there was a break in the rain, they hauled it to the barn.

"Geez, that's heavy," said Megan, massaging her cramping fingers. "We need to find something to set it on."

They decided to check inside the tall cabinets that were built against the back wall. Each of the four cabinets had an image of a different woodland animal burned onto the door.

"Would you like to choose the door with the turkey, the bear, the ten-point buck or the blackbird?" Tony said, sweeping his arm toward them like a game show host.

"Oh, it's so hard to choose," said Megan, playing along. "I'd like to go with, with ... the bear!"

Tony tugged open the door with the image of a black bear. Inside were a few pieces of scrap wood.

"Sorry, Megan," Tony said, still trying to imitate a

game show host, "but there's nothing big enough there to hold your headboard. Would you like to try again?"

"Try the turkey door," she answered, holding her hands together and bouncing on her toes

He dramatically pulled open the turkey door, revealing some old pipes and a pair of dried out rubber boots.

"Oh no, another loser," announced Tony. "But what would you expect from a turkey!? Only two more choices."

"I pick the ten-point buck," said Megan, really getting into the game. "That's got to be a winner."

Tony slowly opened the door to reveal a stack of old, wooden beer crates.

"You win!" he proclaimed. "These lovely crates from Broyhill are the modern way to hold up your headboard."

Megan could hardly contain her laughter.

"Let's see what you could have won if you'd have selected the blackbird door."

Tony reached over and tugged on the handle. It didn't budge. It was locked tight.

"Good thing you didn't choose that door," he proclaimed, "or you'd have gone home with absolutely nothing. Thanks for playing 'The Door is Yours.' Tune in again next week."

Several hours later, Tony made a couple of sandwiches, grabbed two bottles of water and, donning his rain coat, headed out to the barn so he and Megan could have lunch together.

"What a nice surprise," she said. "I was getting hungry but didn't want to go out in the rain. How's the wiring coming along?"

"Seems okay. I won't know for sure until I connect it, but no major problems. How are things in here?"

"Full of surprises. I'm glad that you came down. There's something I need to show you."

She pointed to the carved bird on the headboard.

"I was trying to be very careful stripping the finish around it."

"That's good."

"Well... ." She reached over and pulled the bird straight up, off of the head board. "Turns out it wasn't actually carved from the same piece of wood, like the branches surrounding it. It's a separate piece attached with a couple of wooden pegs."

"That should make it easier to refinish."

"Keep watching."

She flipped the bird over to reveal a hidden compartment on the back, between the pegs.

"This is what I found inside."

She removed something from her pocket, discreetly placed it in the palm of Tony's hand and folded his fingers around it.

Tony remained still for a moment, then slowly unfolded his fingers. Inside was a key.

"So, Mr. Game Show Host, I think it's time for you to reveal what's behind Door Number Four."

"It fits that lock?"

"It does."

"What's inside?"

"I don't know. I waited for you so we could find out together. My guess, it's a dream vacation to Cancun."

They stepped over to the door with the blackbird.

Tony put the key in the lock. It fit perfectly.

He gave it a turn. He could feel the mechanism inside moving.

"You found the key," he said. "You can do the honors."

Megan took hold of the handle and pulled. The hinges creaked a bit as the door swung open.

"Well, that kinda sucks," said Megan, staring at the back wall of the empty cabinet. "You, Mr. Game Show Host, were right. There's nothing here."

"Which sucks more?" Tony laughed, "that there's nothing inside or that I was right?"

"Both."

For some reason, something about the back wall of the cabinet seemed off to Megan.

"I wonder what those wooden strips tacked to the back are for?"

"They look like the sort of strips used to hold up a shelf."

"But then they'd be along the sides, not on the back. And they'd be parallel to each other. These look like the mark of Zorro, if he was a carpenter instead of a swordsman."

"Maybe it's an old board that was reused."

She pulled open the other doors and looked inside. The back walls of these were smooth.

"I feel like I've seen that shape somewhere else. And don't say in an old Zorro movie."

"At least there's nothing creepy or mysterious inside," said Tony. "I don't think we need to add any new twists to The Secret of Blackbird Cabin."

"Which reminds me," said Megan, "how's that book of yours coming along?"

Chapter 14

Now that Tony had the electrical outlets working in the bathroom and bedrooms, he decided they needed something to plug into them.

"Want to come with me to get the wiring kit for the oil lamp? Maybe you could find a couple lamps for the other rooms."

"Sure," said Megan. "I need to pick up some stain and finish for the headboard, anyway."

Their driveway was getting soft due to the all the rain they'd been having. In several low spots, they had to drive through standing water.

"I hate creating these ruts," said Tony. "We're going to have to get some gravel in here."

"Have you looked at the lake, lately?" Megan asked. "I swear that it's several inches higher than it was two days ago. That flat rock that I like to stand on along the shore, it's completely submerged."

"That doesn't surprise me. We're in a natural bowl, here. There's some glacial term for it, but I don't recall what it is. All the water from the surrounding area drains into the lake and then out through the creek."

"Well, it better stop raining soon or the lake will be

over its banks. Do you suppose we should go back to Eau Claire for a while, so we don't end up getting trapped here?"

"Let's see how things look tomorrow. This rain has to let up sometime."

They came home with the oil lamp kit as well as a lamp for each room, along with a few other odds and ends they simply couldn't do without, such as cookies and fresh cheese curds.

Tony brought the oil lamp out to the table so it'd be easier to work on. He'd chosen this particular lamp because it was made of metal instead of glass. He'd be able to drill a hole and run the cord through the empty oil reservoir and out through the base of the lamp, rather than have the cord dangling from the top.

"Megan, could you help me? There's something stuck inside the reservoir and my fingers are too fat to pull it out."

"What about the needle-nose pliers?"

"They're in the toolbox in the car and I don't want to run out in the rain again. I think you might be able to get your fingers in and pull it out."

She was able to fit her index and middle finger through the hole.

"I can feel it," she said. "It feels like a rolled up piece of paper or cardboard."

"Can you get it out?"

"Give me a minute. If I can roll it a bit tighter so it'll fit... There! Got it."

She gently pulled the paper out of the lamp and unrolled it.

"Would you look at that," she marvelled. "It's an old photograph."

She unrolled it flat on the top of the table.

"Bummer," said Tony. "I was hoping for a roll of cash."

The picture showed a happy young couple posed in the open door of an old car. The young man, who had a thin mustache that almost looked drawn on, was wearing a white cotton shirt and light-weight, rather baggy pants. He was sitting on the running board. The smiling young woman, wearing a cute collared blouse was on the seat behind him, her hands lovingly resting on his shoulders.

"That looks like an old Model A Ford," said Tony. "My friend had one when I was in high school. He tried to make it into a hot rod, but it didn't come out too well."

"Who do you suppose the people are?"

"Flip it over," Tony suggested. "I thought I noticed some writing on the back when you pulled it out."

Handwritten in beautiful cursive script were the words: *Sophie & George Jackson, Niagara Falls, June 1931.*

"Niagara Falls," mused Megan. "I'll bet this was on their honeymoon. They sure look happy."

"Why do you suppose it was hidden in the lamp?"

"Darned if I know. Maybe they eloped and didn't want anyone to know they got married?"

"Check out Sophie and George's last name," said Tony. "Look familiar?"

"Hold it a minute," Megan said. "I want to check something."

She stepped over to the Victrola and came back with the 'Bye, Bye, Blackbird' lyrics.

"Look at the handwriting. It's the same. Whoever wrote out those lyrics, penned this inscription on the back of the picture."

"I guess that would make sense. If they lived here, it'd likely be the same person writing both."

"Listen to the lyrics," said Megan:

> *There some **booty** waits for you*
> ***Sugar***'s *sweet, start anew*

"We decided that was a clue to the cash hidden in the sugar bowl, right?"

"Right," confirmed Tony. "And the timetable might have been a way for the person to leave and start anew."

"Agreed. Now listen to *this* line."

> *Check my **bed** and light the **light**.*
> *I'll arrive late some night*
> *Blackbird, bye, bye*

"I found the key when I checked the headboard of the bed," Megan said. "And you just found the picture of Sophie and George because you tried to *light the light*. The only way for someone to light the light would be for them to open up the lamp to replace the wick... and then they'd find this picture."

"This is getting weird again," said Tony.

Chapter 15

During the night, the storm intensified. Lightening lit up the room practically nonstop, with thunderclaps so loud they rattled the windows.

One Mississippi, two Mississippi, Tony counted to himself each time a flash lit up the room. If he made it to *five Mississippi* he'd reassure himself that it had hit at least a mile away. He'd played that game since he was a child. Whenever it stormed, counting *Mississippis* seemed to happen automatically.

Flash!

One Mi... The strike was so close that the flash and crash happened simultaneously.

"Are you awake?" he called to Megan. They were sleeping on the twin beds in the guest room because they'd dismantled their usual resting spot to refinish the headboard.

"Oh, gee, no, I was sleeping peacefully. Why do you ask?"

It was another hour before they finally got back to sleep.

By the time the sun came up, the storm had passed.

"Tony, get up! Come and look outside!"

As usual, Megan was up first.

"We should go out and assess the damage," she said.

"I suppose," Tony said, slowly sitting on the side of the bed and pulling on his socks. "I hope that the solar panels are still on the roof."

It was surprisingly warm and sunny when they stepped out the door.

"What a change," Tony observed. "The storm must have been the trailing edge of the front. Hopefully, that means we're done with the rain for a while."

A quick scan of the horizon showed that the world still existed, relatively unscathed. Several trees were down, one across the driveway, but nothing that he couldn't easily clear away.

Tony stepped a few more yards in front of the cabin, turned and looked up at the roof. *Thank God,* he thought. *The solar panels are still in place.*

"Looks good on the roof," he called to Megan, who had walked around to the other side of the building. "I think we weathered the storm pretty well."

"Ah, Tony. You might want to come back here before you decide that."

He hurried around to the back of the cabin where Megan was once again standing on her favorite flat rock, looking at the lake below her.

"Holy crap!" he said. "Where'd the water go?"

The level of the lake was dramatically lower than it had been before it started raining. The first few yards of the lake were now mostly mud, exposing the milfoil, which was normally hidden beneath the surface.

The pickerelweed and arrowhead plants, that had barely been keeping their heads above the high water a day earlier, were flopped over, their prone position directing one's eyes toward the other side of the lake.

Megan hurried back into the cabin without saying a word and returned a minute later with binoculars. She aimed them where the arrowhead leaves were pointing.

"I think the beaver dam broke," she said, handing the glasses to her husband. "Take a look."

They put on their boots and hiked along the shore to the location of the beaver dam. The sides were still intact, but the center section was gone, the water now flowing unrestricted into the creek. The creek itself had widened out and was littered with sticks and grasses that had been forced downstream.

"Oh man, do you think I caused this by pulling out those branches?" Tony wondered.

"If that was all it took, it'd probably have broken sooner or later anyway."

"Do you suppose we need to build it back up? Notify the DNR? "

"How would I know? We've never had a broken beaver dam before."

"Maybe the beaver will come back and fix it."

"Maybe there's a clue about it in that stupid blackbird song!"

Tony took a deep breath.

"I'm pretty sure the beaver are no longer around. I haven't seen any trace of them while I've been working on the trail."

"You said this is a glacial lake, right?"

He nodded in agreement.

"So obviously the lake was here before the beaver built the dam. Which means that the level it's at now, without the dam, is most likely the level it's naturally supposed to be."

"You're saying that opening the dam was a good thing, returning the lake to it's natural state?"

"Sure."

"Good. I watched a PBS special about beavers a couple years ago and dam building is incredibly complicated. It's all done under water. There's no way I could hold my breath long enough to put this thing back together."

The rest of the day was spent picking up branches and removing the tree that was across the driveway. It turned out there were a couple more blocking their way that couldn't be seen from the cabin, so it was a bigger job than first expected.

By the time Tony got to cutting up the third tree, his chain was getting so dull he practically had to push it through the log.

"I need to get a new chain," he said to Megan as he returned to the cabin, tired and sweaty. "You want to ride along to the store with me?"

A few minutes later, as they were about to get in their car, a familiar pick-up camper pulled into the yard.

"Oh great," said Megan. "I thought we were done with that guy."

Chapter 16

"Hello, there, Mr. Jackson," Tony said, walking over to the pick-up. "What brings you here?"

"I'm just out driving around, looking at the storm damage," he said through his rolled-down window. "Heard there was a washout on your road and thought I'd check to see how you were doing."

"Really," Tony said, not totally buying the story. "And where was this washout?"

"Just past your driveway, where the forest road crosses that little creek. The culvert washed away."

"You're kidding," said Tony.

"Nope, not kidding."

"How'd you get in here, then?" asked Megan.

"The road is open from the east, to Rhinelander and down to Pelican, but if you need to go west to Gleason, you're out of luck. I'm surprised you didn't know about it. It certainly affects you way back here."

"We've been busy cleaning up," said Megan. "I'm not surprised to hear that the creek flooded, though. C'mon. You'll want to see this."

Tony and Megan led their visitor behind the cabin.

"Well, that's different," said Jackson looking at the

lake. "What happened? Did you pull out the plug?"

"In a way," said Megan. "The beaver dam at the head of the creek broke."

"That's probably what caused the culvert to wash out," speculated Jackson.

"Is there a lot of other damage around the area?" asked Tony.

"Seems like the storm kind of hopped and skipped over the area. There are quite a few trees down near Post Lake. Lots of homes without power."

"We had no idea," said Tony. "We probably should have turned on the news this morning."

"Speaking of news," said Jackson. "I happened to catch that story about you guys a few days ago. Made me wish I'd have looked through the place a little better before I agreed to sell it for such a low price. I'd be more than happy to accept a finder's fee, if you're so inclined."

"We haven't decided what to do with it, yet," said Megan, knowing full well that a finder's fee wasn't in Jackson's future.

"Well, just thought I'd mention it. Glad to see that you're safe."

He got back in his vehicle, then pulled someone else's business card out of his pocket and wrote his new phone number on the back.

"If you find anything else I might be interested in, here's my new contact info."

Megan looked at Tony. He knew what she was thinking and answered with a practically imperceptible nod.

"We did find something else that might interest you," Megan said. "Don't go yet. I'll bring it out."

While she went in the cabin, Tony and Jackson compared thoughts about replacement chains for Tony's saw: Husqvarna vs. Oregon vs some unknown brand Tony'd seen on Amazon.

Megan reappeared with something in her hand.

"Sorry to interrupt your captivating conversation, but we found this old picture and wondered if you might be able to tell us anything about it."

She handed the photo to Jackson.

He looked at it, puzzled.

"I'm not sure. The guy looks kinda familiar. Pretty cool car."

"Turn it over."

Jackson read the inscription — *Sophie & George Jackson, Niagara Falls, June 1931* — then flipped it back over and studied the picture more closely.

"I think that's my great uncle George. He was my grandpa's brother. I never knew him, but I've seen a few pictures of him in an old album. With that little mustache, he looks like Clark Gable."

"Is Sophie his wife?" asked Megan. "Since it says Niagara Falls, we wondered if it was taken on their honeymoon."

"As far as I know, George was never married. No mention at all of a woman in his life. He died a bachelor. Now that I think about it, this property might have first belonged to George, before it was transferred to his brother, my grandpa. I really can't say for sure."

"You don't know who Sophie was?"

"Not a clue. But they look like they were pretty close. Let me take a picture of that photo."

Before anyone could object, he pulled out his phone and took a picture of both the back and the front of the old sepia print.

"If I learn something, I'll let you know," he said, handing back the picture. "But I wouldn't get my hopes up. The family never mentions George and they never talk about this place. When I offered to sell it to close the estate, they were more than happy to give me free reign to get rid of it, no questions asked."

"No questions asked!?" said Megan as the pick-up camper pulled out of view. "Sure seems to me like there are questions that should have been asked."

"Yup," said Tony. "And it looks like it's up to us to keep asking them."

Chapter 17

The picture of Sophie and George found its home on top of the Victrola, next to the wrapped-up pile of cash and the police badge. The spot was becoming a tower of clues.

The problem with their tower of clues was that the clues didn't seem to point to anything but themselves.

"I've been reading up on how whodunnit murder mysteries are structured," said Tony, "and I think this might be what's called a closed-circle mystery,"

"Not to question your research, but aren't you missing some things that are kind of important?"

"Like what?"

"Like a murder. And suspects?"

"We've got the dead body."

"Which probably didn't actually exist."

"But do we really need a body? The clues on the lyric sheet pointed to the stolen money in the sugar bowl. So we've got a crime."

"But that mystery's been solved. It was the money from the bank robbery."

"But the robber was never identified. We don't know who done it. That's kind of important in a whodunnit."

"Maybe George was the robber," suggested Megan. "He and Sophie look like Bonnie and Clyde wannabees. Put a couple of Tommy guns in their hands and they're ready to head out on a robbery spree."

"I can't tell if you're serious or mocking me."

"A little of both, I guess. We might as well have fun with it."

"Speaking of fun," said Tony. "I bought some things to help us solve our mysteries. Wait here."

He went outside. Megan could hear the car door open and close. When he returned he was carrying a couple of shopping bags.

"Okay," he said. "I stumbled upon a couple things at Goodwill and couldn't resist."

He pulled a Sherlock Holmes style hat out of the bag.

"Did you get his cape, too?"

"Couldn't find one. But I did find this."

He revealed a beautiful, brass magnifying glass, complete with a table-top stand.

"That is actually pretty nice."

"It'll be handy for looking at details. Maybe we'll notice something important in the picture of George and Sophie. It would have come in handy when we were trying to make out the image in the center of the badge."

"What'd you get for me? We're in this together, after all."

He reached further into the bottom of the Goodwill bag and pulled out a strand of pearls.

"Those are beautiful."

"Yup, just like Agatha Christie always wore."

"You do remember that Agatha wasn't actually the detective solving the murders in her books? That was Hercule Poirot."

"I know that," he answered indignantly. "But I thought that you, *mon amie*, would look rather silly with a little, waxed mustache."

"What else have you got in that bag?"

"You know how in TV shows and movies they're always putting up pictures and clues and connecting everything with string?"

He pulled out a stack of multi-color Post-it notes, a roll of kite string and a box of push pins.

"You've really decided to get into this," remarked Megan. "I'm impressed."

"Are you in?"

"Sure, why not."

"I saved some big cardboard pieces from the solar panels. We can stick the notes on there and then connect them with strings."

Tony wrote in big, bold letters across the top, Board of Clues.

"Let the mystery begin," said Megan.

They soon began sticking notes to the board. As each was posted, they explained aloud why it was there.

• **Dead Body:** Supposedly discovered by a hunter some years back, but may have simply been imagined by a young Fred Jackson.

• **Fred Jackson:** Sold us this cabin cheap because he said there had been a body found here. Seems rather shady.

• **Grandpa Jackson:** Property was sold to settle his estate.

• *Secret hiding spot behind the kitchen cabinet:* Location of the sugar canister with a pack of cash and a RR time table inside.

• *Stash of cash:* Money from 1932 bank robbery that had not been recovered. One bank robber, of four, was never caught or identified.

• *C. & N. W. Timetable:* Shows the schedule of trains between the Northwoods and Chicago; summer 1932.

• *"Bye, Bye Blackbird" record:* Found on Victrola where it would be easy to discover. Flip side, seems to be purposely scratched.

• *"Bye, Bye Blackbird" Lyrics Sheet:* The variations from the actual song lyrics seem to be clues: So far the sugar canister stash, the key in the headboard and the photo inside the lamp.

• *Police Badge:* From Chicago C. &. N. W. division. Might have belonged to Grandpa Jackson. Found with trash under cabin.

• *Picture of Sophie & George Jackson:* Found hidden inside lamp. George is brother to Grandpa Jackson; he may have first owned this property. Who is Sophie? Unclear from inscription on back of picture if her last name is Jackson.

• *Key in headboard:* Found by accident, but alternative Blackbird lyrics seem to have been a clue. The key opened the empty blackbird cabinet in the barn.

"Can you think of anything else?" asked Megan, studying their newly created Board of Clues.

"There're already more clues there than I realized. The

other strange thing that's happened since we've been here is the lake suddenly losing water."

"The only suspect for that is Mother Nature," laughed Megan, "and I think we can leave her off the board."

"So," said Tony, "is it time to get out the string and see how these fit together?"

"Let's look at it again another time," advised Megan. "I was hoping to finish the headboard this afternoon. It only needs one more coat of poly and then we can bring it back in. What's on your agenda?"

"I should continue working on the trail around the lake. We'll probably need a bridge, now, to get over the creek."

"Which reminds me," said Megan, looking at their newly expanded shoreline, "we'd better start cleaning up the bank near the cabin. The seaweed that's in the mud is starting to smell. I noticed a few dead frogs, too."

"How about I work on the trail while you finish the headboard and then, after supper, we can work on the shoreline together."

"Well," said Tony after he and Megan had finished a relaxing picnic supper of brats, potato salad and cole slaw, "do you still feel like cleaning up the lake shore?"

"Not really. How about we just relax tonight?"

"I was kinda hoping you'd say that," Tony said, stretching the sore muscles in his neck and arms. "Tomorrow, we can start fresh."

* * * * * *

The sun had been shining brightly for an hour by the

time Megan and Tony were awakened by the racket outside.

"The birds certainly are making a lot of noise this morning," Megan grumbled.

She looked out the bedroom window.

"Tony, you've got to see this."

Tony peered out the other window at a sea of blackbirds.

"There must be hundreds of them," Megan guessed.

"Same thing on this side," Tony said, looking out a different window. "They're everywhere."

"It's like a scene from 'The Birds.' I wonder what's going on?"

They went to the door, opened it and cautiously stepped a foot or two outside. The chirping was ridiculously loud. Very few of the blackbirds were in the air. They were busy scratching and digging, kicking up leaves and grass.

"Looks like there's a blackbird convention going on here," said Megan.

"I've heard about this happening," said Tony. "There's even a name for it, something like a hallucination of blackbirds."

"I could easily see why someone would think they were hallucinating. This is freaky."

The birds surrounding the building were oblivious to the bare-footed humans who had stepped a few yards further out in the yard.

The humans, on the other hand, were astonished at what they were witnessing and couldn't take their eyes of the multitude of shiny, black bodies.

"They don't seem dangerous," said Megan above the

din. "Should we try to chase them away?"

"I'm not running out there into that sea of feathers," Tony responded without hesitation. "I saw the movie."

Watching the undulating waves of birds was almost hypnotic. They were not only in the grassy areas, but also digging through the leaves in the woods.

"There must have been a hatch of something that they're going after," said Megan. "Maybe because of all the rain and then the hot sun?"

The two watched for another few minutes, transfixed, then went inside to get dressed.

As if on cue, through the bedroom windows, they noticed the birds start to leave. Hundreds flew up into the air at once, a highly choreographed cyclone of wings. By the time the couple had finished dressing, the birds were gone. The landscape still and eerily quiet.

"That was an interesting start to the day," said Megan as she spread some jam and cream cheese on a slice of bread.

"Murmuration," said Tony, who had been searching for something on his phone.

"What?"

"A murmuration. That's what it's called when the birds all come together like that. Listen to this:

In many cultures, blackbirds are often associated with mystery, magic, and transformation. A flock of blackbirds can symbolize a sense of mystery, change, or even a warning. In literature and mythology, blackbirds have been used to represent various themes such as death, prophecy, and the unknown.

"Well, that's comforting," said Megan. "I guess Mother Nature was mad that we left her off our Board of Clues."

Chapter 18

Megan began raking away the decaying grass and sea-weed from around the large, flat rock where she usually stood. The water was now low enough that she decided to clean up the area around the rock so she could sit on it and dangle her feet in the cool, clear water.

The tiny lake was obviously spring fed. It had kept its level at the new depth since the dam broke. They weren't sure how deep it was in the middle, but it seemed to drop off quickly.

Tony was working further up the shore, just beyond the barn. He had his waders on so he could stand in the lake as he pulled out the myriad of intertwined branches that had fallen into the water over the years.

Some of them, near the surface, were rotted and broke off in his hands. Others, along the bottom, held strong, buried in the sand. The wet and slimy wood kept slipping out of his grasp.

This isn't working, he thought. *At this rate, I could be here all day.*

He recalled seeing a long-handled, iron pole with a hook on the end among the garden tools piled in the cor-ner of the barn. He wasn't sure what it was originally for, but thought that it might be just what he needed to get a bit more leverage on the stubborn branches.

With the pole in hand, he stood on the bank, where he had better footing, reached the pole out over the water as far as possible, and let the hooked end drop to the bottom. After a twist to make sure he'd snagged something, he pulled it in, towing the pile of branches that he'd caught onto the shore.

He soon found a rhythm to his reaching and retrieving. The only problem with this technique was that he churned up so much mud that the once-clear water had become a murky brown and he had no way to see what he was aiming for. Finding and hooking the branches was purely a matter of luck.

Nonetheless, he soon had a respectable pile of brush draining alongside the shore. It was nice to have proof of his efforts beyond the pain in his arms.

This would have been so much easier thirty years ago, he thought, laying the pole on the ground.

He decided to take a break to see how Megan was doing.

"Looking good," he said as he walked up behind her.

She'd made noticeable progress clearing the area around the flat rock and was now using a rake to clean up the gravel and sand that surrounded it in the water.

"I think this will be clear enough to wade around in," she said. "The bottom isn't mucky at all. If we can bring in some sand, we could end up with a nice little beach."

"I'm going to grab a snack," said Tony, heading for the cabin. "Would you like something?"

"No thanks. I'm good."

Tony grabbed a snack for himself, then went back to where he was pulling branches out of the lake. The water was once again crystal clear and he was happy to see that there were very few branches left at the bottom. His drop and drag method had been working well.

Never one to quit before a job was completed, he decided to pull the last few branches out before going back to work on the trail.

He tossed the rod out and dropped it directly in the center of the biggest branch still remaining. This one was buried in the sand. He gave it a tug and it barely moved. He tugged again. This time it came up a few inches. One more, extra-strong pull and it suddenly broke free, toppling Tony onto his backside, feet in the air. He glanced toward Megan.

Glad she didn't see that, he thought, quickly getting back on his feet.

He dragged the branch out of the water to the pile and discovered that this wasn't a branch that had broken off and fallen into the water, it was a small tree that had been growing on the shore and toppled over. It still had its roots.

That's an interesting piece of wood, he thought, keeping it separate from the other branches. *I might be able to build something fun out of that. It could make an interesting lamp.*

The water was so churned up, now, that he couldn't see if there were any branches left. He decided to toss the hook one more time to see if there were any that he'd missed.

Instead of the usual splash followed by silence as the

hook settled onto a branch or the lake bottom, this time he heard a splash followed by a plink. He gave the pole a twist and a tug. He'd hooked something, but it was held fast. He pushed the rod out a bit farther, then pulled it back quickly.

Plink.

He tried again.

He had definitely found something solid.

A rock? No, it sounded like it was metal.

It was small enough that he could easily get the hook under it.

But tug as he might, it wouldn't budge.

He repositioned the pole and was able to catch it from a slightly different angle. This time when he pulled, he could feel the hook slide along the side of whatever it was he'd found. It was long and skinny.

From the sound it made, it was metal.

He put on his waders and walked back into the lake, churning up even more dirt. He reached down until he found the object. It was a pipe, maybe an inch and a half in diameter.

He followed the pipe about another foot into the lake, where it stopped, propped on a large rock. He held his hand against the open end and could feel water, colder than the lake, flowing out of it.

Puzzled, he followed the pipe back all the way to the shore, where it disappeared into the bank.

"Megan," he called. "When you've got a minute, come over here. I've found something puzzling."

"I was hoping we were done with puzzling," Megan said as she walked over to Tony, who was still standing in the murky water. "What'd you find? And don't even think about telling me it's a dead body."

"There's a pipe under here. I seem to have found the source of the water for this lake."

"Okay, that makes no sense. Lakes don't get their water from pipes."

"Unless the pipe is coming from a natural spring. People used to do that all the time; drive in pipes around springs to make it easier to get the water."

"Of course," said Megan. "Like the spring in Chippewa Falls. They've been getting water out of that spring house for a century and selling it all over the world."

"Want to help me follow the pipe and see if we can find a spring house? Maybe we could start our own spring water bottling business."

Chapter 19

Tony stood in the lake at the end of the pipe and sighted to where it was buried in the bank.

"Megan," he said, "grab a stick and walk over to the edge of the trees and I'll tell you to stop when you're in line with the pipe."

She moved several feet to her left. "Stop right there," he instructed, "and poke the stick into the ground."

She placed the stick a few inches into the loam.

"Can you feel anything there? Did you hit anything?"

"No. But it's mostly rotted leaves and roots here. I can't push it in very deep."

"Okay. I'm coming out and we'll try again."

When he reached the shore, he placed a tall stick into the spot where the pipe disappeared into the bank so he'd have a reference point for further sightings.

"I'm going to switch out of these waders," he said, "and then I'll join you."

While Tony changed into his work boots, Megan began searching the area for any sign of an old spring house. They were at the base of the hill in which the back end of the barn was buried.

She went up the hill a few yards, staying in line with

the branches they'd stuck in the ground. Another two steps and her foot stuck something metallic buried under the leaves.

She kicked the leaves away with her toe.

"Looks like someone was using this hillside for target practice," she said as Tony joined her. She showed him a rusty old bucket she'd uncovered. It was shot full of holes.

"Jack and Jill couldn't fetch much water in that," he joked. "Put another branch there to mark that spot, then go up to the top of the ridge and I'll let you know if you're staying in the sight line."

She went another dozen yards and he told her to stop.

She looked around her on all sides, then kicked at the leaves. Her toe hit something metallic.

"I think I found another old bucket."

She pushed the leaves aside with her toe, then bent down and carefully uncovered the object with her hands.

"It's not a bucket," she said. "It's some sort of a vent pipe coming straight up. Looks like it used to have a cover over it, but that's pretty much rusted away."

She knelt down close to the cast iron pipe and placed her ear near the opening..

"Shhh," she said as Tony clumped his way up the hill to her. "Listen."

She motioned for him to put his ear next to the pipe.

"It sounds like water running."

"That's what I thought," she said. "This must be where the spring starts."

"Do you see any trace of a spring house?"

While Tony searched the area around them, Megan removed the debris immediately surrounding the vent.

"There's a pile of rocks surrounding the pipe," she said.

"Maybe that was to keep it in place," speculated Tony. "Or to keep it from collapsing."

"Or to keep it from being found," said Megan. "A pipe this size sticking out of the ground would draw attention, but a pile of rocks... "

"... wouldn't even be noticed," finished Tony.

"Why hide a spring house?"

"Good question. Let's see if we can dig down and figure out what we're dealing with."

They quickly discovered that the tools they had on hand weren't adequate. Tony decided to look around in the barn to find something that would be up to the task.

While he was gone, Megan searched the area around the vent pipe. She found another rusted out bucket, and an old glass jar, but no other objects.

Tony came back with a post hole digger, a grub hoe and a long-handled shovel. He also found an old metal rod that he thought could be used to probe down into the soil to locate solid objects; to help them figure out where they should dig.

Megan used the shovel to clear away the debris directly around the vent while Tony used the posthole digger and rod to probe the surrounding area. As far as he could ascertain, there was something solid about three feet deep on all sides of the vent. As he went down the hill toward the lake, he could no longer locate it. The same was true when he probed further into the woods. As he probed closer to the barn, however, he kept hitting whatever was buried beneath them.

"I'm uncovering something solid," Megan called. "I think I've found the top of the spring house."

Tony hurried over with the probe. Sure enough, all the way around the vent he hit something solid.

He picked up the grub hoe and continued deepening the hole that Megan had begun with the shovel.

What he found were paving bricks, somewhat arched.

While he continued uncovering the bricks, Megan walked across the top of the ridge toward the barn. She noticed something curious: The top of the ridge was level and free of any large trees from the vent to the barn wall; the wall that was buried in the hillside.

"Tony," she called. "Bring those diggers over here. I think the spring house extends all the way to the barn."

Within a few minutes, Megan's hunch was proven correct. A few feet from the barn wall, Tony was able to expose the arched brick top of the structure.

"This thing is huge," he said, standing up and pacing off the distance to the vent pipe. It's at least thirty feet long. Way bigger than would be needed for a spring house. What do you suppose it's for?"

"A better question," posed Megan, "is 'how do we get inside?'"

Chapter 20

"The opening has to be along the back wall," said Megan as they stepped inside the barn. "There must be an opening hidden behind those shelves and cabinets."

"Let's start with the blackbird door," said Tony. "It's the only door with a lock, so it seems the most likely candidate for a hidden entrance to the spring house."

While Tony began tugging on the shelves to see if any of them would come away from the wall, Megan stepped over to the blackbird door and pulled on the handle.

"Well, that was dumb," she said, frustrated. "I didn't realize the door locks automatically. I took the key to the cabin and hung it on the Board of Clues. I'll be back in a minute."

While she was gone, Tony checked the other cabinets.

First, he opened the door with the wood burned image of the bear. He removed the pieces of scrap wood that were inside, exposing the wooden back wall. There was no handle, latch or doorknob visible. He knocked on the back wall. It felt and sounded solid.

Next he opened the turkey door. The old boots and pieces of pipe where right where he'd first seen them.

Looks like leftover pieces of pipe from the spring.

He removed everything from the cabinet, stepped inside and checked the wall for latches or handles. Nope. He pounded on the back. Solid.

"I checked two of the other cabinets," Tony reported to Megan when she returned. "I took everything out and no hidden door leading to the spring house."

"It's got to be in here somewhere."

"Next up is the ten-point buck," he said. "It was our winner before, so keep your fingers crossed."

The wooden cases that Megan had used to hold the headboard hadn't been put back inside, so there was nothing to remove.

"No winner this time," Tony announced after banging on the solid back wall.

"Which leaves us with the blackbird door," said Megan, putting the key in the lock.

"This has to be the way inside," said Tony. "That's why there's a lock on the door."

Megan gave the key a turn and dramatically pulled open the door, revealing ... nothing.

"Still no trip to Cancun," said Megan.

Tony stepped inside.

"I don't see any handles or latches."

He banged on the back wall. It sounded hollow.

"Okay, that's a good sign," he said. "The others all sounded solid."

"Do you see any sort of latch or handle?"

"Nope."

"What about those slats of wood tacked to the wall? The ones that look like the mark of Zorro."

Tony took hold of the middle piece and gave it a tug.

Not much to grab on to. The ends were a bit loose, but it was solidly attached in the center."

"Try the other two slats," said Megan"

"They're barely attached at all," he reported. "Just a single screw near the ends. They're more or less just hanging there."

He tried pulling on them as door handles, but the only thing that happened was the free end of the lower slat dropped down an inch or two. It reminded him of the trick handle on the kitchen cupboard.

He tried rotating both of them further and discovered that with a bit of effort he could spin each of them around until they hit the center slat.

"They didn't build these very well," said Megan. "Anything they'd try to hang from them would fall right off."

"I think they built them exactly the way they intended."

With two hands, Tony twisted simultaneously on the top and bottom slats, using them as levers against the middle board, which began to pivot on its center pin.

Tony could feel something inside the wall release. With barely a push, the back of the cabinet swung inward. A gentle whoosh of damp, musty air rolled out of the darkness.

Neither said a word, then Megan broke the silence. "I can hear water running. Can you see anything?"

"Not a thing. It's pitch black in there. I can't even see the floor."

"Don't go in," Megan cautioned, taking hold of Tony's shoulder. "The floor might be slippery."

"I'll go up and get a lantern," said Tony.

"Tomorrow," said Megan. "We've had our share of surprises for one day."

Tony, agreeing, stuck a piece of wood in the secret doorway to keep it from closing.

"We should probably shut the blackbird door," said Megan. "We don't need any critters sneaking in there during the night."

Tony closed the blackbird door, making sure to leave the key in the lock.

* * * * * *

The next morning Tony gathered together their lanterns. They had a couple of small flashlights and two LED camp lanterns.

"The batteries in these lanterns are practically dead," said Tony. "We need to get more batteries before we explore the spring house."

"We could use some groceries and a few other things, too" said Megan. "Let's go in together and we can get everything in one trip. And maybe grab some lunch while we're out. Maybe stop at Goodwill."

"I'm getting the sense that you aren't real eager to explore the spring house this morning."

"Gee, that obvious?"

Tony just laughed.

"I think I'm ready for a break," she admitted. "We keep discovering new things and each is more mysterious than the last. It's exhausting."

"I'm good with that. It's supposed to be in the nineties this afternoon. Maybe by then we'll appreciate a nice, cool tour of the spring house."

* * * * *

Later that afternoon, they stepped into the barn carrying their fully charged lanterns and a couple of miniature spotlights they'd picked up that they could wear on their heads.

"Ready for Pee Wee's next big adventure?" joked Megan as she turned the key in the blackbird cabinet door.

Tony gave a firm nod. "Lights. Camera. Action!"

"You know, that would have been a good idea; to bring a camera. If we find something really strange we could send it to one of those weird ghost hunter shows. I wonder if they pay for those clips?"

Tony stepped into the cabinet and pushed the door open all the way.

They switched on their head lamps.

"Yowsers!" said Megan. "This is not what I was expecting."

Chapter 21

The space was much larger than either of them expected. The light from their head lamps struggled to reach the end of the web-covered chamber.

"We're going to need the lanterns," said Tony, stepping back through the hidden entryway. A moment later he returned and handed one of the lanterns to his wife.

The floor was covered with rough-cut planks showing wear down the center.

The walls on either side were lined with wooden shelves reaching from the floor to the arched-brick ceiling, which was about seven feet high in the center. Several rusty kerosene lanterns hung from a hook close to the entrance, their glass chimneys raised, ready to assist those who needed to make their way into the dark and dank cavity.

"This looks like a creepy movie set," said Megan.

"I doubt that a movie set would smell this musty," said Tony. "Do you suppose it's safe to breathe in here?"

"I think we'll be okay. I can feel some air moving. That pipe has probably kept it fairly well ventilated."

A salamander scurried onto their path, stopped and stared at them, its eyes shining bright. Having never seen a human before, it meandered off under the floor boards, unconcerned.

They took a few steps farther into the chilly underground room. The only sound was water running, coming from the far end, where they could make out a tiny glow, probably sunlight filtering down through the newly uncovered vent pipe.

They moved ahead cautiously.

Aside from a few empty wooden cases, like those Megan had used to support the headboard, the shelves on this end of the cavern were empty.

About halfway down, there was a break in the shelving on their left. An alcove, built of the same brick as the rest of the structure, extended back about ten feet. In it was an assortment of copper tubes, pipes and kettles, neatly piled and stacked.

"Looks like parts of an old still," Tony speculated, the beam from his head lamp darting around in the pile. "I remember reading that there were bootleggers up here during prohibition. Some were connected to Al Capone."

"Do you suppose Jackson knew about this?"

"Hard to say. He doesn't seem to know much about anything."

Just past the alcove, the shelves were no longer empty. Stacked side by side, two deep, were crates with brownglass bottle tops showing.

Tony handed his lantern to Megan, put his hands on one of the crates, gave it a wiggle to warn away any critters that might be hiding behind it, then easily pulled it down and set it on the floor.

The bottles were uncorked and empty.

Megan aimed her head lamp back into the shelf where the case had been removed.

"The case in the back looks like it has bottles with caps on them. Can you reach in there and pull it out?"

Tony reached into the shelf and grabbed the wooden crate. It was considerably heavier than the one he'd already removed.

"You're right," he said. "These bottles are full."

He slid it to the edge of the shelf, then carefully set it down on top of the first crate.

Megan lifted one of the dust-covered bottles out of the crate.

"Oh, my. Look at this."

She held up the bottle so Tony could see the label that was beginning to peel off the side.

Prominently pictured on the center of the label was a silhouette of a blackbird, superimposed over a background of stylized pine trees. Above it were the words:

Old Blackbird Whiskey

Beneath the image:

170 Proof
For Medicinal Use Only

"Well, I guess that explains all the blackbirds," said Megan. "It's nothing but branding. Like people who have beer signs or Coca Cola stuff decorating their house."

Tony reached down and pulled out another bottle and studied the label.

"Good to know, but I have to admit, it's kind of disappointing. Now all the mystery is gone."

"They might be worth something," Megan speculated,

putting the bottle back in the case. "I read a story a while back about a couple who found bootleg whiskey hidden in the walls of their house, and they sold it for, like, a thousand dollars a bottle."

"Nice."

He started sliding the empty crates to the side, one by one, so he could see what was behind them.

There were about a dozen cases with full bottles hidden behind cases with empty bottles."

"Wow," said Megan, quickly doing the math in her head. "At six bottles per case, that would be seventy-two bottles. If we can find a buyer for them, we've nearly paid for the cabin!"

"Can you imagine Jackson's face when he hears about this?" said Tony. "He's definitely going to be asking for a finder's fee."

"I don't think so," laughed Megan. "Technically, it appears that Jackson sold us liquor without a license. Isn't that illegal?"

Tony laughed. "And he could also get a hefty fine because he didn't card us."

"Good point. Because we look so much like minors."

"With these lights on our head, we do look like miners." Tony joked.

At the very end of the walkway, in the far right corner, was the spring. An outlet near the top of the masonry trough that collected the water kept it from overflowing.

"That must be where the pipe to the lake begins," said Tony.

The water rose up from the bottom of the well-built concrete basin. It was about the size of a bathtub, but sunk down below the level of the floor. The depth was hard to determine because the light from the lanterns reflected off the surface, making it difficult to see the bottom.

"Turn off your lantern," Tony suggested, doing likewise.

The focused beams from their head lamps revealed the crystal clear water to be several feet deeper than the floor.

Megan ran her fingers through the gently moving liquid.

"It's really cold," she said, flipping a few drops at Tony with her fingers.

Tony dipped his hand into the chilly liquid, then retaliated by playfully splashing water into Megan's face.

"You dork!" she shouted, jumping back, slipping on the wet floor and crashing against something behind her that was hidden in the shadows.

Tony turned toward her, the beam of his head lamp redirecting his gaze. The grin on his face vanished.

"Holy shit!" he muttered.

Tony reached out, grabbed Megan's hand and pulled her toward him. She turned her head and screamed.

Propped in the corner was a human skeleton, dressed in a white, short-sleeved shirt, wearing a pair of old cotton pants. A large knife, stabbed through a piece of paper, was protruding from its chest.

Tony switched on his lantern. Megan slid behind him, her hands around his waist.

"Looks like Jackson was right," said Megan. "But the hunter never found him. He's still here."

"We'd better call the police," said Tony. "Don't touch

anything. This is now a crime scene."

"Wait a minute," said Megan, shining her head lamp onto the skeleton's arms and hands. "I think it's fake. There are wires and bolts holding it together."

Tony stepped up to the figure for a closer look. Sure enough, the bones were held together with bolts and nuts. The jaw was held in place with tiny brass springs.

"It sure looks real," he said, putting his finger on the chin and moving the jaw up and down.

"It must be a Halloween prop," said Megan.

"A very good one."

Tony pulled the knife out of the chest and unfolded the piece of paper it had been holding in place. There was writing inside.

"What's it say?" asked Megan.

He read the note silently to himself, then read it out loud.

Enjoy your visit to St. Peter.

I'll be watching you.

"Isn't that what Jackson said he overheard his grandpa saying when he was a child?"

"Something like that."

Beneath the message was a large letter *Z*, written like the mark of Zorro.

Megan looked closely at the note in Tony's hand, then stepped around him and touched the skeleton's skull.

"It's not plastic. I think it's a real skeleton."

She focused her light on the side of the skull.

"There's a label here. As best as I can make out, it says:

CLAY-ADAMS CO.
New York
Medical Skeletons
S - 6025

"I think it's a model skeleton that would have been used in a medical school."

"That's a relief. I'm glad we don't need to call the police to investigate a murder."

"Do you suppose this could have been used to scare people away from their bootleg operation?"

"Possibly. He's not dressed very scarey, though. Looks like George in that picture we found in the lamp."

"Look at this," said Megan, shining the light just above the skeleton's teeth. "Someone took a pencil and drew a little mustache on the skull. Just like the mustache George has in the picture."

"You don't suppose George died and they sold his body to a medical school?"

"Seriously? Then how'd it get back here? Besides, it's not a real skeleton."

"Well, actually, I think it is," Tony speculated, running his finger nails against the bones. "Somebody wanted it to look like George."

"Not only look like him, but to point out that George had been killed. And how."

"Do you suppose Z is the killer?"

"The killer wouldn't leave such an obvious clue to their identity."

"Good point," Tony said. "But someone who witnessed the murder might leave a clue like that, hoping the authorities would find it."

He placed the note and the knife in his pocket.

"I think we've found enough clues for one day," said Megan. "Let's go back to the cabin and start adding strings to our Board of Clues."

"What about the skeleton? Do we just leave him here?"

"I don't think Georgie Boy is going anywhere."

Chapter 22

"Time to add a few more Post-it notes," said Megan, leaning the Board of Clues against the table so they could easily work with it.

"The newest addition," she said, writing the title on a note and explaining it as she stuck it to the board:

• ***Spring House:*** *Hidden behind a locked, secret door, bootlegging operation.*

"The next addition is... ," said Tony, handing Megan a note on which he'd written:

• ***Old Blackbird Whiskey:*** *Discovered in Spring House. Many full bottles hidden behind empty cases.*

The next items they added were:

• ***Skeleton:*** *Found in spring house. Made to look like George Jackson. Probably a medical model.*

"Should we include the knife?" Megan asked.

"Probably not a bad idea. I didn't really look at it. But murder weapons are always important clues in whodunit mysteries."

• ***Knife:*** *Stuck in skeleton's chest, holding note.*

"By the way," Megan asked as she wrote, "how's that novel of yours coming along?"

"Working on it as we speak," he laughed. "Just haven't

gotten around to putting much down on paper."

"Speaking of paper. We can't forget this."

She jotted down on another sticker:

• ***Note on Skeleton:*** *Similar to comment overhead by Jackson as a child. Seems like a threat.*

"Add that it was signed by '**Z**'," said Tony.

A light went on in Megan's brain. "Hold that thought." She stepped over to the Victrola and, after removing the clues stacked on top, pulled out the "Bye, Bye Blackbird" record.

"I knew this seemed familiar," she said, holding the flip side up to Tony. "Look at the scratches. They're in the shape of a '**Z**.'"

"That can't be a coincidence. What's the song that '**Z**' obviously doesn't want us to hear?"

"It's called 'That's Why I Love You.'"

Tony wrote and posted the note:

• ***"That's Why I Love You":*** *Flip side of "Bye, Bye Blackbird." Damaged by "Z"? Why?*

"I think '**Z**' should get their own note," Megan said. She wrote,"

• *'**Z**': Scratched on record. Signature on skeleton note.*

"Don't forget the shape of the secret latch inside the blackbird cabinet that opened the spring house door," added Tony.

"Good one," said Megan, adding the info. "I'd forgotten about that."

Tony studied the board.

"You know what else we haven't written down? ***Blackbird.*** Even if it's just advertising for their booze, it sure pops up a lot. He posted:

• ***Blackbird:*** *Whiskey brand logo, also appears various other places.*

They sat back and studied their handiwork. There were nineteen notes posted on their Board of Clues.

"Kinda overwhelming, isn't it?" Megan said. "Connecting these is going to be an interesting challenge."

"Let's go pick up a pizza," Tony suggested. "We'll think better with full stomachs."

Instead of getting a carry-out pizza, they decided to treat themselves to a relaxing meal at Pizza Hideaway, their favorite local restaurant, hidden back in the woods.

Carrying a doggy bag with what was left of their large, Hawaiian Deluxe pizza, they walked in the cabin door.

"Ready to get started?" Tony asked as they entered the living room.

"Gee, can't you at least let a girl get in the mood?" Megan joked, elbowing him in the side.

Tony walked over and picked up the Sherlock Holmes hat and Agatha Christie pearls that Tony had found at Goodwill.

"We might as well look the part."

He wrapped the string of pearls around her neck and put on the deerstalker hat.

She looked around the room. *Still not right,* she thought.

She lit one of the old oil lamps and placed it on the table so that the warm, yellow light flickered over their Board of Clues.

"Now," she said, "let's get this show on the road."

Okay," said Tony, a length of string in his hand. "Where do we start?"

"Let's start with the dead body, since that was the first thing we heard about."

Tony poked the pin in the Dead Body note and tied the string to it.

"We can connect this to Fred Jackson," he said, stretching the string to Jackson's note. "He's the one who told us that a body was found here."

"I think we should also connect the body to the skeleton," added Megan. "That might be what the conversation was actually about that Jackson overheard when he was a kid."

"Then we should also connect the skeleton to Grandpa Jackson. And Grandpa Jackson to Fred Jackson."

Tony placed more strings.

"This is going to get really confusing," he said.

"I'm going to start a list of questions we have about each of these clues," said Megan.

She found a pad of paper and a pencil and began writing.

"The first question I have is, *Who was Grandpa Jackson?* We need a first name for the guy."

"We also need to know when he took ownership of this property. Fred Jackson mentioned that it might have first belonged to George."

"Which means we also need to connect Grandpa and George."

"That makes sense, since they were brothers."

Tony stuck a pin in the picture of George and Sophie and connected it to Grandpa Jackson.

"Should we also connect him to Fred Jackson?"

"No. Fred said he'd never met George. Which means

George must have died either before Fred was born or when he was quite young."

"Which raises another question for the list," Megan said. *When did George die?*"

"What about Sophie? Should she have her own note?"

"Let's leave her with George for now. The picture shows them together, so linking their notes would be redundant."

"Not to mention, this is already going to be one crazy mess of string when we get finished. I can see why the clue boards in the crime shows always look so cluttered and messy."

They continued for the next hour, trying to link the clues together. The secret hiding place in the kitchen easily linked to the stash of stolen cash and to the train schedule and also to the clues on the alternative 'By, Bye Blackbird' lyrics, which in turn seemed connected to the picture of George and Sophie hidden in the lamp and to the key hidden in the headboard, which opened the lock in the blackbird cabinet that led to the secret entrance to the spring house.

"I may not have enough string," said Tony. "I had no idea how complicated this would be."

"Here's another question," said Megan, who was already on the second page of her list. "Why was the flip side of the record damaged? Were there clues in the lyrics to "That's Why I Love You" to whatever crime it is that we're trying to figure out?"

"Which raises the most important question," said Tony. "What crime are we trying to solve?"

Chapter 23

"That was an interesting exercise, last night," said Megan the next morning. "But now I'm even more confused than I was before we started trying to tie everything together on that stupid Board of Clues. Would you be okay with not doing that again? Ever."

"Absolutely! Last night I dreamed I was trapped in a room with lots of doors and no matter where I tried to go, strings kept appearing, tangling me up."

Megan laughed.

"Those clue boards have to be made up by the movie prop departments. I can't believe they're used in real investigations."

"Are we wasting our time trying to figure out what happened here?" Tony asked. "This isn't turning out to be the relaxing cabin by the lake we were counting on."

She thought for a moment.

"I have to admit, I'm rather enjoying the mystery of it all. It's not boring up here, that's for sure. But I do think we should quit using that board. The hat and pearls should probably go, too," she added with a smile.

"The list of questions you wrote down was a good idea. We're good at finding answers to questions we have."

"Sometimes almost obsessively so," she laughed. "You do know that once we start wondering about something, we aren't happy until we find the answer."

Megan's telephone rang.

She looked at the name of the caller.

"It's the guy from the coin shop," she said to Tony, then answered the call.

"That's interesting. ... We haven't decided if we want to sell it or not. ... We'd need to talk it over. ... Sure, if we decide to, we'll get back to you. ... Thanks for letting us know."

"Was that about the money?" Tony asked.

"Somebody's interested in buying the badge. He didn't give them our info, just told them he'd check with us."

"I suppose, that way he knows he'll get a cut if we sell it."

"Do you think we should?"

Tony thought for a moment, then answered confidently: "Lets keep it. It's a pretty cool knick knack. If we need some extra money, we've got the cash from the robbery."

"Don't forget the whiskey," said Megan. "That might bring a good price."

"Good point," said Tony, returning to their previous train of thought. "No sale on the badge. Now let's make a plan for answering the questions on your list."

"We can start at the top and work our way down," said Megan, picking up her list. "The first questions are: *Who was Grandpa Jackson?* and *When did he become owner of our property?*"

"We could probably get that info at the court house. The register of deeds office should have the names of the property owners going all the way back. What's the next question?"

"*When did George Jackson die?*"

"That might tie into the property ownership. Could we assume that Grandpa took over the property when George died?"

"Not sure we should assume that, but it'll get us a start."

"How about one more question for now?"

Megan read: *What are the details of the bank robbery and the money hidden in our wall?*"

"Those sound like enough questions to start with. How about we split up finding the answers? I'll take the info about the property ownership and Grandpa and George Jackson, and you can search for info about the bank robbery. That sound okay?"

"Sounds like a plan."

After lunch, they drove into town. Megan went to the public library while Tony headed over to the court house. They agreed to meet back in an hour at Ted's Dairy Bar to share what they'd learned and then reward themselves with a sundae.

Megan settled herself at one of the public computers and started by searching the databases of local newspapers, looking for bank robberies in the 1930s.

It didn't take her long to find a news article about a bank robbery that took place June 2, 1932.

Bingo, she thought after a quick scan. *This has to be the robbery the coin shop guy was referring to.*

She made a copy of the article and highlighted the sections that seemed most pertinent.

Three Bandits Now Face Court Charge

Three of four robbers who held up and looted the First National Bank of Sun Lake, Mich. are under arrest and will be charged today with armed robbery.

All but about $2,000 of the loot has been recovered.

Those arrested are John and Rudolf Davis, brothers, and Frank Jacoby.

The Davis brothers confessed to authorities that the robbery was planned by a man from Illinois that they met a week earlier at a Northwoods resort. They said he was known to them only by the name "Chicago Blackie."

The gang was driving a brown Oldsmobile sedan.

They entered the bank at 10:30 a.m., robbed it and sped away. The back window of the sedan was shot out and nails strewn on the highway as the car sped toward Wisconsin.

Officers from neighboring communities were alerted and joined the chase.

Witnesses said that at the Michigan-Wisconsin border the officers were less than 10 minutes behind the robbers' car.

The gang eventually left the main highway and took to smaller roads through the woods, trying to elude police. This led to their getting lost and they abandoned their car.

The Davis brothers and Jacoby were quickly tracked down and arrested.

The fourth robber, believed to be from Chicago, is still on the loose.

At the court house, Tony found himself searching through actual paper documents. He began by scouring old plat books, looking for the correct parcel of land. He kicked himself for not having brought along the legal description of their property, since that was how everything was organized.

After several false starts, he finally found the correct map. By carefully studying the forest roads, he was able to locate the lake that was part of their property. With that info, he was able to determine the legal description needed to narrow his search.

On a plat map from 1910, the property in question was listed as belonging to the Brady Lumber Company.

He checked the parcel on a map from 1930. The property was then listed as being owned by a G. Jackson.

Got it! thought Tony.

He jumped ahead to the 1935 plat book.

The ownership had changed. It was then listed as belonging to a Z. Jackson.

Confident he was on the right track, Tony asked to see the deeds that were registered for that particular parcel.

At the top of the stack of documents was the original copy of the deed he and Megan had recently filed.

This would have been a lot simpler if I'd have thought to bring along a copy of our deed.

Below it in the stack was a simple, handwritten quit claim deed dated August 7, 1932. Title to the property was transferred from George Jackson to Zachary Jackson.

Grandpa's name was Zachary Jackson.

Z. Jackson.

Z.

Chapter 24

They enjoyed their sundaes in the park near the Dairy Bar as they exchanged what they'd learned.

"I'll bet that the robber, the one who wasn't caught, hid out at our cabin," said Megan. "He was from Chicago. The Jackson family was from Chicago. Maybe they were friends."

"Or," Tony posed, "George Jackson was Chicago Blackie. We'd wondered before if George might have been the robber."

"That makes sense," said Megan.

She thought for a moment.

"Here's another idea: The robber is lost in the woods. After a few days, weak and hungry, he stumbles upon this hidden bootlegger's cabin. To keep him from giving away the location of their still, the bootleggers kill him, hide his body in the spring house, keep the money for themselves and hide it in the wall until it's safe for them to spend it."

"Apparently, though," said Tony, "that safe time never came. The money stayed in the hidey hole until we found it. And the skeleton in the spring house couldn't be the robber's, it's a medical model."

They both were silent for a minute as they worked their way to the bottom of their sundaes.

Tony finished first and broke the silence.

"George and the robbery have to be tied together, somehow. He seems to have disappeared about the same time. The records show that the same year as the robbery, the property was transferred to George's brother, Zachary Jackson."

"Maybe George helped the robber hide the money, then the robber came back for it later, killed George and hid his body in the spring house."

"Except, same problem as before. The money was still in the wall. Why would he kill George without finding out where the money was hidden? Not to mention, the body in the spring house was a medical skeleton."

Megan crumpled her napkin and tossed it into the nearby trash can.

"We're proving the old saying that 'the more you know, the more you know how little you know.' Time to go back and work in the yard. It's much too beautiful a day to spend another minute indoors researching a mystery that doesn't want to be solved."

"I need to pick up some spikes, chain and a come-along on the way home," said Tony. "This is a perfect day to work on the bridge where the beaver dam washed out. My goal is to get the trail around the lake completed by the Fourth of July."

"Let's stop at the nursery, too," said Megan. "While I was at the library, I also did a little more research on deer resistant plants to put in around the cabin and along the shore. Everything's on sale right now."

* * * * *

For the next couple of days, Tony and Megan enjoyed sprucing up the area surrounding Blackbird Cabin and around the lake. Tony continued clearing the trail and cut some cedar posts to use for the bridge, while Megan worked her landscaping magic around the cabin.

If either of them had thoughts or theories about the mysteries they'd uncovered, neither of them mentioned it to the other. They'd purchased their cabin on the lake to be a peaceful and relaxing little oasis, and both were determined to make that a reality.

At least that was their plan.

"Megan," said Tony, out of breath and soaking wet. "You need to come and see what I've found beneath the old dam. Bring your phone."

Megan followed him along the edge of the lake until they got to the creek, where the beaver dam had been.

"I've been pulling out the old dam so I could pound in the footings for the bridge, and I came across this at the bottom."

He pointed to a pile of old, chewed-off branches, still dripping with mud.

"Is that a... ?"

"I think so. I can see now that there are a bunch of bones mixed in with the branches. I didn't even notice them at first. They were woven in with all of the other sticks and logs that were holding everything together.

"When I pulled out the last section of the dam, the water began rushing faster and knocked me over. I put my hand down to catch myself and braced myself on a rock. Only it wasn't a rock. There were holes in it. I could feel the teeth. I pulled it out of the water and set it there next to the pile. Then I came to get you."

Megan stared at the skull. The jaw was missing. No bolts, springs or labels.

"I think you should take some pictures," said Tony. "This one is not a medical skeleton."

Chapter 25

A sheriff's deputy was the first to arrive. No flashing lights. No sirens. No CSI team or cadaver dogs. Just a young man in a khaki uniform with a holster on his hip.

Tony walked him out to the dam and showed him what he'd found.

"Definitely appears to be human," the deputy said, pointing out the obvious. "Looks like it's been here awhile."

"So, what happens now?," Tony asked. "Do we have to contact a funeral home or what?"

"I believe that our department can have a team come out to investigate the scene and retrieve the body. Or what's left of it. I'm not aware of any cases of someone missing in the area. By the looks of the remains, though, this probably goes way back, before my time."

"We were wondering if it might be connected to an old bank robbery," offered Tony.

"What bank robbery?"

"In Michigan in 1932. One of the robbers was never found. Maybe this is him."

"Sure. Good tip. I'll pass that along to the crime scene folks. Maybe they'll be able to identify it. Probably not, though. They usually look at stuff like blood spatter, bullet trajectories, stuff like that. You don't really have any useful clues to work with here."

He began stretching some yellow tape around the area.

"This area is now off limits. Don't disturb anything else until the scene has been processed," he said matter of factly. "We'll take it from here. I don't believe that you have any cause for alarm, but make sure you keep your doors locked, just to be on the safe side."

He jotted down a few things in a notebook as he headed back to his vehicle.

"We'll be in contact if we have any questions," he said as he buckled up. "The crime scene unit will probably be here in the morning. Thank you for contacting us."

"That was worthless," Tony said to Megan after the deputy's vehicle disappeared through the trees. "He didn't seem even slightly curious about who it might be or why it was here."

He switched into his best Barney Fife voice.

"Hi. I'm Deputy Doofus. My first question is, why did you bother calling me when I could have been doing something important like catching speeders."

"You're still mad at them for catching you in their speed trap last year, aren't you?"

"Hey, they had four cop cars hidden behind the hill, all lined up and ready to pounce on innocent drivers. But they send one junior high deputy to investigate a body being found."

"Just as well that it's low-key."

"Whatever. I hope they don't take too long to wrap this up. I was making pretty good progress on the bridge."

* * * * *

The next morning two black vehicles pulled up in front of Blackbird Cabin: an SUV and a cargo van. Crime Scene Response was painted on the side of each.

Two investigators wearing black T-shirts with State DOJ Crime Lab boldly printed on the back, stepped out of the vehicles and introduced themselves.

While one of the investigators talked with Tony, jotting down the details of how he found the skeleton, Megan led the other, armed with a camera, to the dam. She took numerous pictures of the scene, even setting little numbered sandwich boards next to the skull and visible bones.

After placing the skull in an evidence bag, the two of them began methodically sorting through the piles of branches that Tony had pulled out of the dam, separating out a number of bones and placing them in a plastic tub. Then they moved into the water, searching for additional bones that were still caught in the mud and branches.

"It's a lot more interesting on TV, isn't it," Tony said quietly to his wife.

"Kind of reminds me of weeding the garden," she responded. "I'm glad that I didn't find any bones when I was cleaning up around the flat rock."

Megan and Tony stood back and watched for a while longer, then realized they were of no use to the investigators and went back to the cabin where they could keep track of things from the comfort of their lawn chairs behind the cabin.

They'd barely gotten comfortable when another vehicle pulled up. They heard a car door open and close. Assuming it was another police vehicle, they stayed in their seats.

"Hello again," said a familiar voice a minute later. "Dawn Hogan, I did the story about the cash you found hidden in your wall last month."

"Sure" said Tony, standing to greet her. "You did a nice job putting that together. We learned a few things from your report that we hadn't known before."

"Thank you," said Dawn. "Glad that you found it helpful. So, what have we got going on here today? The only info I have is that the crime scene unit was sent out to investigate a body found in a lake. As soon as I heard where it was, I recognized it as your place. There's not a lot of other cabins out here. Could we talk?"

"Sure," said Tony. "Why not."

"It's not really a body in the lake," Megan explained as Dawn set up her camera. "It's just a skull and parts of a skeleton that washed out from under an old beaver dam. Looks like it's been there a long, long time."

"Which explains why the investigators seem so calm and there's no ambulance here," Dawn observed.

"Correct," said Tony. "No need for a stretcher. They're putting what's left of the body in a plastic tote. It's just bones that were tangled up in the branches."

"That's interesting," said Dawn. "Do you think there's a connection to the remains and the money from the robbery that you discovered hidden in your wall?"

"We really don't know," said Megan. "That seems like a possibility. We're hoping that the investigators can tell us more about who the person might have been."

Dawn noticed that the investigators appeared to be packing up their equipment.

"Excuse me a minute," she said. "I need to shoot some B-roll of the investigators while they're working. Hopefully, I can get a comment from them, too."

When Dawn was out of hearing range, Tony asked Megan, "Do you suppose we should say anything about the spring house?"

"Let's keep that to ourselves for now. We don't really need any more film crews out here."

"At the rate things are going," Tony speculated, "the station'll probably offer us an ongoing segment. I can see the promo now: 'Tune in every Wednesday for the latest installment of What's New at Blackbird Cabin, brought to you by Bob's Furniture Barn.'"

As Dawn was packing away her tripod and camera, one of the investigators came over to talk with Tony and Megan.

"I thought you'd appreciate knowing that, based on our preliminary findings, its likely that the body has been submerged for many years, probably decades. We'll know more after we do some tests, but I wouldn't worry about your safety."

"Can you tell us anything about the person?" Megan asked.

"We were able to find quite a few of the bones. Enough to make us believe that the person was probably a male, probably in his mid twenties."

"Can you tell how he died?"

"We didn't immediately notice anything to indicate

gunshot or knife wounds. But, as I said, we'll know more after we conduct some tests."

"How about an educated guess?" asked Tony.

"My guess is—and don't you dare tell anyone that I'm guessing—is that the person drowned and was washed under the dam when the dam was much smaller. Maybe in a storm like the one that breached it a few weeks ago. All of the mud that was packed around it helped preserve the bones. If you hadn't been trying to put in that bridge, the body likely would never have been found."

Tony noticed the other technician removing the yellow tape.

"Am I okay to work back there again?"

"It's all yours. If you come across any more bones or artifacts, please save them for us."

"If I find anything, we'll get them to you right away," Tony assured the investigator.

"No need to rush. As I'm sure you can understand, this will be a low priority investigation, so I wouldn't anticipate the lab working on it for quite awhile. Get it to us when you can. Cases like this sometimes take years."

Dawn's story aired that night. The couple was pleased that she didn't sensationalize it or give the precise location of their cabin. The last thing they wanted was curiosity seekers invading their private little paradise.

Chapter 26

Tony had barely begun working on the bridge the next morning when he heard a vehicle in the driveway. He looked up to see Jackson's camper.

Megan stepped out of the cabin.

"I saw the news last night," Jackson said as he exited the truck. "Looks like I was right, after all."

"Except for the part about the body being found a number of years ago. By a hunter. Behind the barn."

Jackson shrugged his shoulders.

"Why don't you go over to the dam and talk with Tony," Megan said. "He can fill you in on what he found."

Tony wasn't thrilled to see that Megan had passed the man off to him.

"If you want a finder's fee, you're too late," grumped Tony. "The CSIs took the whole body. Didn't even leave us a finger bone."

"Good to see you, too," said Jackson, holding up his hands. "I come in peace."

"Good," Tony said, picking up a sledge hammer. "You can help me set these footings. Hold that post while I pound it in."

Jackson squatted down and grasped the newly peeled

cedar post, his arms extended as far out as he could reach. Tony positioned the sledge hammer back over his shoulder, then swung it forcefully toward the top of the post. Just as it was about to make contact, Jackson chickened out and pulled his hands and arms away. The post slipped off center and the gigantic hammer skidded along its side and into the mud.

"I could have done that better alone," Tony groused. "What brings you out here today?"

"Saw the news about the bones and was curious." He straightened the post and held it tightly. "Give it another whack. I won't let go this time."

Tony swung the hammer again, hitting the top of the post perfectly, forcing it down a good eight inches.

"Thanks," said Tony. "I should have it from here."

He gave it several more strong pounds until only about three feet remained above ground.

"They said you thought it might be the bank robber?" Jackson commented.

"Just a guess. But things don't really add up all that well."

"Such as?"

"For one thing, if it's the robber, who killed him and why?"

"Probably for the money."

"But the money was left in the cabin. Why kill someone and then leave the cash? The cabin belonged to your grandpa, right? Did he seem like the kind of guy who'd kill someone?"

"Maybe. I know I was always scared of him."

"You were right, by the way, about this place first belonging to George. I checked it out and the deeds confirm that he owned it for several years before the title was transferred to a Zachary Jackson."

"Zachary was my grandpa. I always thought his name had a great sound to it—Zachary Jackson—it just sort of rolls off the tongue. But people never called him Zachary. Not even Zack. He went by the nickname Zee."

"Zee, like the letter *Z*?"

"Uh huh."

"There's something I think you should see." He set down his sledge hammer. "Come with me."

Megan was surprised to see Tony walk into the cabin with Jackson.

"Have a seat," Tony said to their guest. Megan looked at him, the obvious question posed via her eyes.

"Jackson just confirmed that Zachary was his grandfather."

"We'd already figured that out."

Tony looked from Megan to Jackson. "Tell him what he was called."

"Grandpa's name was Zachary, but he went by the name Zee. What's the big deal about that?"

Megan understood why Tony'd brought him inside. She walked over to the Board of Clues and removed the note they'd found impaled on the skeleton and handed it to Jackson.

Jackson read it aloud: *"Enjoy your visit to St. Peter. I'll be watching you. Z."*

"What is this?" he asked.

"Maybe you can tell us," said Tony. "You said that your grandpa threatened you by saying that if you told anyone about a body, you'd get to visit St. Peter. Am I right?"

"Pretty close. Why'd you write this note?"

"We didn't write it," said Megan. "We found it stuck in the chest of a skeleton."

"Seriously? Why didn't the CSIs take it?"

"It wasn't that skeleton," Tony said. He turned to Megan. "Should we show him?"

She thought for a moment, then nodded.

"You need to come with us to the barn."

"Hey, I was just curious. No need to do anything you'll regret."

He stood up and turned toward the door.

"I'll just get in my truck, drive away and make believe I never stopped by."

Tony was between him and the door.

"Seriously, I'll never pester you again," said Jackson.

Tony shook his head. "We want you to see something."

"See what?"

"It'll be easier to show you than try to explain." Tony stepped over to the Victrola and took the knife from the pile of clues. "Megan, would you grab the lanterns."

Jackson considered making a run for the door, looked at the knife in Tony's hand and changed his mind.

"We're going to the barn," Tony said, motioning toward the door. "You first. We'll be right behind you."

Jackson obediently stepped through the door, considered a quick dash to his truck, then decided to simply walk toward the barn, as calmly as possible.

"Sure is a lovely day," he said, maintaining a reasonable distance between himself and his captors.

When they reached the barn, Megan scurried ahead

and opened the door.

It took a few seconds for their eyes to adjust after being out in the bright sunshine.

"Okay," said Jackson, scanning the nearly empty room, "what's in here you want me to see?"

"Not here. There's another room hidden behind those cabinets," said Megan. "We're going back there."

"Seriously," said Jackson. "Just let me leave. I promise I'll never come back."

"We're not holding you prisoner," said Tony, realizing that Jackson had the wrong idea of why they were taking him to the spring house. "We simply want to show you something that we found. You might be able to help us figure out what to make of it."

Megan turned the key to the blackbird cabinet door and pulled it open, switched on her lantern and stepped through the second door, which was still propped open with a piece of wood.

Tony switched on his light and motioned for Jackson to follow Megan.

"What the... ?" Jackson said under his breath as he entered the damp and musty space. The only sound was the water trickling from the spring at the end of the tunnel-like room.

"It's at the far end," said Tony. "C'mon."

Jackson spied a bottle of whiskey that was sitting on the shelf and stopped.

"I've seen one of these before," he said. "In my cousin's office. He has it displayed in a little glass case, on the shelf behind his desk."

"What's your cousin do?" asked Megan.

"He's a distributor. Alcohol. It's been a family business for a couple generations."

"Well," said Tony, "this may well be where that business began."

Jackson picked up the bottle. "It's still full. This is worth a few bucks. Very rare. Be careful with it."

"There's plenty more where that came from," Tony said, indicating the no-longer-hidden cases of filled bottles stacked on the shelves. "But that's not what we brought you here to see. Wait here a second, I want to reset the scene."

Tony hurried to the spring and replaced the knife with the note in the skeleton's chest.

"Okay, come down here. Watch your step, the floor is slippery."

Tony stood in front of the skeleton to hide it from view, then stepped aside for Jackson to see.

"What the... . Who is that?"

"No one," said Tony. "It's a medical skeleton—so I guess it actually was someone at some point—but not someone who died here."

"Look at the way it's posed," Megan directed. "That note we showed you, we found it here, just like that, stuck to his chest with the knife."

"Does it remind you of anything?" asked Tony.

"No. Should it?"

"Remember that old photo we showed you of the young man and woman sitting on the Model-T? You thought it looked like a picture you'd seen of your great uncle George. This skeleton seems to be posed to look like it's George. Same shirt. Same pants. Even a little mustache."

"You're sure it's not actually George?"

"The skeleton's held together with wires and screws and there's a tag on the back of the skull," said Megan, "so unless George donated his body to science, it's not him."

"But someone appears to want us to think it's him," said Tony.

"Seems that way," said Jackson. "What did the police say?"

"We didn't tell them. They had their hands full with a real skeleton."

"Do you think this was put here to let someone know that the skeleton in the lake is George?" asked Jackson.

"We are hoping you might be able to tell us," said Megan. "It's your family."

"No one talked about George. Aside from the few pictures I've seen, no one ever mentioned him."

Megan looked at Tony. He nodded imperceptibly.

"How would you like to join us in finding out what happened here?" asked Megan.

"You opened the door to this mystery," added Tony. "Seems only fair that you should step through it, too, and help us solve it."

Chapter 27

Megan, Tony and Jackson sat around the table, staring at the Board of Clues.

"We'd hoped to never look at this thing again," said Tony, "but it might help you get an idea of the various clues we're looking at. A new set of eyes might help us figure out what it all means."

"Wow," said Jackson. "That's overwhelming. Can't say that I'm particularly happy seeing my name up there."

"You're definitely part of the puzzle," said Tony.

"I suppose. How do you think I could help?"

"You mentioned a cousin," said Megan, "the one with the Old Blackbird Whiskey bottle. Could you check to see what he knows about this place? Maybe he can point us in a direction we couldn't discover on our own."

"The only time I've seen him in the last ten years was at Grandpa's funeral," Jackson responded. "The whole family turned out. People I've never seen before. My cousin and I were never very close. He was on the side of the family that, quite honestly, kind of scared me."

"Any chance you saved the memorial folder from the funeral?" asked Megan. "That would list family members who died before he did."

"I don't think I saved it, but I doubt it would tell you much. Pretty much everyone died before Grandpa did. He was over a hundred years old."

"Did your grandpa leave an old family bible? People his age often kept track of births and deaths in their bibles."

"He didn't have much stuff left. He'd been in the nursing home for years. His house was cleaned out when he was moved there."

"What about the photo albums you remembered looking at when you were a kid; the album where you saw the pictures of George? Any idea where they ended up?"

"There were several albums set out at the funeral for people to page through. I don't know who ended up with them. It might have been my cousin. He's the one who organized the funeral and burial, which didn't take much thought since Grandpa's grave had been waiting for him in the family plot since forever."

"Could you check out the family plot?" asked Tony. "If you could find George's headstone, we would know when he died and that he's buried there. That would rule out that the skeleton in the lake is him. Will you be going back down there soon?"

"I didn't have any plans to. I don't spend much time in Illinois. Most of my family is in that cemetery plot and I have no wife or kids."

"Not to be nosy," said Tony, "but where do you live? You never gave us a business card or anything with your address on it."

"Right now," said Jackson, nodding toward his camper, which was visible through the window, "there."

"Do you have a lot around here?" Tony asked. "Seems

like half the summer residents in the Northwoods come from Illinois."

"I have a half acre on a lake about thirty miles from here, with a garage, electricity, water and septic. I considered taking over this cabin when the family said they wanted to get rid of it. All I knew about it was that the place was condemned and no one was allowed to go up here."

"It's not that bad," said Megan, defensively.

"I see that, now that I've been here," Jackson continued. "Supposedly there was an old family curse or something. No one would tell me what that was about. To be honest, I don't think anyone knew. No one had set foot on the property for a long, long time. Since I was up here, I offered to get rid of it for them."

"Why didn't you just move in here yourself?"

"I could see as soon as I pulled in that there was no electricity, no water, no sewer. I didn't need more land. So I decided to stick a note on the bulletin board at the store and see if someone would be interested. Seventy-five grand was more appealing to me than paying taxes on a second piece of property that I didn't need. I'm only up here in the summer. I have a lot in Arizona where I park in the winter. I set aside the cash I got from you so I can buy a better camper."

Tony steered the conversation back to the topic at hand.

"Are you willing to help us figure out what happened here and whose skeleton they just fished out of the lake?"

"I can't think of any reason to say 'no.' This is more interesting than my usual days."

"That's great," said Megan. "When can you start?"

"I could go down to Chicago and check out the cemetery this weekend."

"Fantastic."

"While you're down there," added Tony, "do you think you might be able to discreetly ask your cousin what the market is for a case of hundred-year-old whiskey?"

"That all depends," smiled Jackson. "Will there be a finder's fee?"

"Let's see how things fall together," Tony grinned. He went to the cupboard and pulled out a bottle of Old Blackbird that he had cleaned up and handed it to Jackson.

"Consider this your down payment."

Chapter 28

"Was that dumb of us to recruit Jackson's help?" Megan asked Tony after the camper had disappeared into the trees.

"We'll find out. It wouldn't surprise me if he sells the whiskey in a parking lot somewhere and never goes to Chicago."

"Nothing would surprise me. The whole Jackson family sounds rather suspicious. We shouldn't have gotten involved with any of them."

"Woulda, shoulda, coulda," recited Tony. "The three most useless words in the English language. If you think about it, we didn't get involved with them. They got involved with us when they sold us the cabin. No going back at this point."

Tony went inside and grabbed a bottle of Gatorade.

"I'd like to get another hour's work in on the bridge this morning, before it gets too hot. When I'm done, how about we drive up to that antique store that's way back in the woods, the one with such weird hours? They might be open today."

"Sounds like fun. Let's grab a couple subs on the way through town and eat them at the river overlook."

The antique store was open! They'd only been there once before, at least two years ago, so they had no idea what they might find. The last time they were there, Tony discovered a seventy-five-year-old lap steel guitar that he'd repaired and vowed to someday learn how to play.

They snooped around in each of the small buildings.

"This birch bark art is amazing," said Megan to her husband. "Do you think we could make something like that? We've got some birch trees on our land.

"We could probably learn how on YouTube. I think the trickiest part is knowing how and when to remove the bark without killing the tree."

Tony picked up an old grub hoe that also had an axe head on it.

This is exactly what I need for clearing the trail, he thought, checking the price tag. Nine dollars! *You are coming home with me.*

He worked his way through the maze of funky junk, being careful not to snag anything with his tool.

He caught up to Megan in the next building. She was standing next to a Gramophone, holding an old 78 rpm record.

"Tony, you won't believe what I found. It's 'Bye, Bye Blackbird.'"

"The same as the record we have?"

"Yes, except this one isn't ruined on the flip side. I'd like to hear what that song sounds like. Maybe there'll be some clues in the lyrics."

"There's no way we can get away from this mystery, is there?"

"Doesn't seem like it."

She gently clutched the fragile record as she continued browsing.

The last building was surrounded with garden art. Among the statues, bird baths and whirligigs were a number of old, rather small grave markers.

"What's with the headstones?" she asked the owner as they were checking out. "Doesn't seem like the sort of thing one would find in an antique store."

"A buddy of mine sells memorials. Those are some of his samples and mistakes. There doesn't seem to be much of a market for sample headstones. I'll give you a really good deal if you're interested. Ten bucks, your choice."

"No thanks," said Megan. "But we appreciate the offer."

"I'm surprised you didn't take another look at the headstones," Tony said as they got back in their car. "You always seem to come up with interesting ways to use things that no one else wants."

"Like you?" she joked.

When they got back to the cabin, Megan could hardly wait to play her new record.

She carefully placed it on the turntable with "That's Why I Love You" facing up. She cranked the handle a half dozen turns and flipped the switch. Once the platter was spinning, she gently set the needle on the record.

When skies were gray, you came my way,
That's why I love you, that's why I love you.
I learned to smile, like sweethearts smile,

That's why I love you,
Who wouldn't love you?

In a world, a happy world of sunshine,
Life's content since heaven sent you here.
I'll confide I never saw the sunshine,
Not until your heart was mine, my dear.

When skies were gray, you came my way,
That's why I love you, I do.

"What a sweet and catchy tune," Megan said. "It's almost like on this side of the record they fall in love, and then, on the other side, they have to say bye, bye. Who would destroy such a beautiful sentiment?"

"Based on the Zorro shape of the scratch," Tony speculated, "I'm thinking the answer is Z, The next question is 'why would **Z** destroy such a beautiful sentiment?'"

"Maybe love didn't come his way?"

Chapter 29

"Jackson called while you were in the woods," Megan said to her dirty and sweaty husband. "He's actually made some progress down in Chicago."

It had been five days since they'd last seen their new partner in crime hunting.

"What did he discover?"

"First off, he talked with his cousin. He said he was eager to show him the bottle of Old Blackbird Whiskey. Unfortunately, the cousin wasn't as excited as he was. In fact, he said his cousin was pretty annoyed that he'd sold the place without first discovering and removing the stash in the spring house."

"I can see how that might be. But that's his problem. We bought the place 'as is' in good faith."

"That's what I told him and he agreed. Nevertheless, he did get some information from his cousin about the whiskey. Do you want the good news or the bad news first?"

"That doesn't sound very promising. Start with the bad news."

"The bad news is, we can't sell it... ."

"What!?"

"Let me finish. We can't sell it because we do not have

a liquor license. We can drink it, look at it and imagine that it's worth a fortune, but it is against the law for us to sell it."

"That's pretty crappy. What's the good news?"

"His cousin is willing to sell it for us on consignment."

"With what sort of arrangement?"

"It would be a three-way split. The distributor would keep fifty percent and we would get forty percent."

"Let me guess. The other ten percent goes to Jackson as a finder's fee."

"You got it. I told him we'd need to talk it over, but I don't see that we have any other options. Jackson said he'd be willing to deliver it to Chicago in his camper."

"Hopefully, he won't charge us per mile."

"I didn't ask."

"Did he go to the cemetery?"

"He did, but he said something seemed odd. All of the stones in the family plot are similar, with the exception of George Jackson's. His is smaller, made of a different kind of stone, and the poorly carved message doesn't match any of the other inscriptions, which are things like Beloved Mother and Wife or info about military service. George's stone simply says 'Bye, Bye Blackbird' and the dates, 1906-1932. He was only twenty-six when he died."

"Wow, he died young," said Tony. "That's about how old he looks in the picture with Sophie."

"Which explains why Sophie doesn't show up as part of the family. He must have died before they could get married. That's the sad side of the Blackbird record."

"I wonder how he died," said Tony. "It must have been some sort of accident."

"Maybe the still exploded. That would explain the pile of scrap metal in the spring house and behind the barn."

"For someone so young, an accident seems a likely cause. He looks healthy in the picture."

"At least we know it wasn't George you found in the lake."

"Which puts it back to being the bank robber," said Tony. He thought for a moment. "I'll bet that the robber showed up looking for a place to hide. Something went wrong and George killed him, maybe accidentally, and dumped his body in the lake. Then George hid the money in the wall, but before he could use it, he was killed in an explosion."

"Makes as much sense as anything else," said Megan. "How do our other clues fit in to that scenario?"

"Sophie was staying here at the cabin with George," Tony speculated. "She was so devastated by the loss of her lover that she destroyed the happy side of her record."

"I could see someone doing that," said Megan. "Maybe in our obsessive search for clues, we're imagining that three random scratches on the record, made in a spontaneous act of grief, looks like the mark of **Z**."

"Good job!" announced Tony, holding up his hand to high-five his wife. "The mystery of Blackbird Cabin has been solved."

She began to raise hers in response, then lowered it.

"That's too easy," she said. "It doesn't explain the skeleton with the note stuck in its chest. That was not a spontaneous act of grief. That took some serious planning."

Chapter 30

Before they agreed to the consignment deal with Jackson's cousin, Megan wanted to know more about what they had found. She decided to do some research on bootlegging in Wisconsin.

She began at the history museum. She knew they'd recently done a program on bootlegging and was hoping to pick the director's brain, without giving away too much about their situation.

Much of what she learned was expected. There definitely was a Northwoods connection to the Chicago mob. The museum's collection included a letter from Al Capone to a land developer in the area requesting information about procuring a well-hidden piece of property that included a good source of water.

The Capone letter didn't say what the land would be used for, but Megan had a pretty good idea.

She found no mention of the Jackson family or their connections, but it seemed possible, likely even, that they'd have worked with Capone. Or, maybe, against him.

She came across a couple of old newspaper clippings that especially intrigued her.

One essay was by an older woman recalling stories she'd heard from her parents about stills in the area. She explained that the stills were typically cobbled together out of copper vats, copper tubing, and sheets of tin. They were located deep in the woods where they couldn't easily be found. A source of good water was essential.

Sounds an awful lot like our place, thought Megan.

The next article that caught her attention was about a murder that took place in 1932, not in the Northwoods but in southeastern Wisconsin in an area called the Holy Land. It was called the Holy Land because the tiny villages in that part of the state had names like Mount Calvary, Marytown, Jericho and St. Peter.

The Holy Land was also known during prohibition for it's bootlegging activity and connections to John Dillinger's gang.

The article included the story of a man who was posing as an investigator for the Chicago police, convincing the Holy Land bootleggers that he'd remain quiet about their activities for a cut of their profits.

It didn't take long before the bootleggers discovered his charade. It was believed that they or their partners in Chicago had captured the imposter in the village of St. Peter and taken him north by train, where he was killed and buried somewhere in the woods. His body was never found.

* * * * *

Megan returned to the cabin clutching a handful of copied newspaper articles.

"Tony," she said excitedly. "I think I discovered who you found in the lake. Read this."

She handed him the article about the bogus investigator.

He read it carefully, then scanned back over it again.

"This is fantastic," he said. "Sure sounds like it could be our guy."

"I'm thinking that they drowned him in the lake and destroyed his clothes. There were no clothes found with the skeleton, right?"

"Right."

"The badge that you found atop the trash under the house; that was probably his."

"The coin guy said that was an authentic badge, not a fake."

"Nothing says he didn't steal a real badge to look more convincing."

"Did you notice where this happened? The village of St. Peter. The comments Jackson overheard as a child probably referred to what happened there."

"I can see how a kid could be confused. Do you think we need to pass this info on to the CSI folks?"

"I don't want to wait two years to possibly find out what happened here."

"What should be our next step?"

"I'd like to find out where the skeleton in the spring house came from. That might help us figure out who put it there."

"The label on the skull includes the name of the medical supply company and some sort of number," said Tony. "Maybe they're still in business and have records of serial numbers. Kind of like checking the serial number to find out when and where a vintage guitar was built. I've checked the Fender site a couple of times."

"Good," said Megan. "Since you have experience in that sort of research, you're in charge of finding out about the medical skeleton."

"I can do that," said Tony.

"While you're doing that, I'd like to try finding out who our police badge originally belonged to. As I recall, William at the coin shop said the badge numbers were unique to the officer who wore it. He might be able to point me in the right direction."

"Let's plan to go into town tomorrow and see what we can learn."

* * * * *

Tony took his laptop to the community college student center, which overlooked the lake, where he could log into their wifi network. Megan chose to begin her research at the coin shop, and then, if needed, use the public computer at the library.

They met up ninety minutes later at the dairy bar to compare notes on what they'd found. This time Megan tried a raspberry shake, made with fresh raspberries, never syrup, while Tony stuck with his old standby, a chocolate and butterscotch sundae.

You start," said Tony. "What did you learn about the badge?"

"Not much. William Kunze confirmed that the numbers on the police badges are typically unique to the officers, but there's no publicly accessible database of those numbers. He thought we'd have our best luck requesting the info about a specific officer, then trying to find that person's badge number."

"We could begin by asking for Zachary Jackson's badge number. That would either rule him out or point the finger at someone else."

"It's not that easy. To do that, we would need to file an official Freedom of Information request with the police department, but unless we know exactly what we are requesting, such as a specific document for a specific date and precinct, it's unlikely that we'd get a response. Unlike a university, government agencies aren't in the habit of helping people with their research.

She continued: "I also read that while badge numbers were unique, there wasn't necessarily any pattern to how they were issued. As far as I can tell, the same badge number might be issued to a different person if the first person who had it was no longer with the force."

"Sounds like jersey numbers on a sports team," said Tony. "Unless the number is retired, it can be used again and again by different players."

"That's how I understand it. What we do know for sure is that the badge was of the style used in the 1930s. It says right on the badge that it's from the Chicago & Northwestern Railroad division, which, if we can believe what Jackson told us, is where his grandfather served."

"So we're back where we started."

"Looks that way. We sure don't want to file a Freedom of Information request."

"Agreed," said Megan. "How about you? What did you learn about medical skeletons?"

"Quite a bit, actually."

"Great. Who is sitting in our spring house?"

"It was probably some homeless person whose body wasn't claimed," said Tony. "That's about as specific as I can get."

"That's not much help."

"Not so quick. Before we left this morning, I took a couple of pictures on my phone of the skeleton—minus the knife and note—and a close up of the skull showing the name of the company and the serial number."

"Good planning."

"Thank you."

"The Clay-Adams company no longer exists. However, there is now a private museum in New York that specializes in medical skeletons."

"You're kidding."

"Seriously. They just opened this year. You can tour the place for twenty dollars. Their goal is to educate the public about this unique industry.

"I looked at their website and found pictures of a skeleton that looks just like ours. It was dated from 1927. The serial number on ours is 6025, so I guessed that it's from 1925."

"That puts us in the correct time period."

"Right. Then I noticed in the museum's contact information that they promised to respond to inquiries within twenty-four hours."

"And... ?"

"I emailed them the pictures I'd taken and am hoping

for a response. The young man who is running the museum seems very dedicated and enthusiastic. I watched his video about how medical skeletons have changed over the years, which was pretty interesting. I'm optimistic he will respond."

They decided to run a few errands before heading home. On their way out of town, Tony abruptly turned into the driveway of the college."

"I want to check my email," he said.

"They sat on the student center patio and Tony booted up his laptop.

He had a response from the director of the museum:

Thank you very much for your inquiry. The pictures that you sent were very helpful. Your guess about the date is correct. Your articulated skeleton was most likely prepared in 1925. It's a male, about 25 years old. According to the records we have, it was sold a year later to a nursing school in Chicago. We have no record of what happened to it after that as the school closed in the early 1930s.

If you decide that you do not wish to keep your skeleton, we would be happy to negotiate a fair price. We look forward to seeing additional pictures without the clothing. (Sorry, that sounded bad.) Thank you for contacting us.

John Terry, director

Chapter 31

"Maybe that nursing school had a going out of business sale," quipped Megan, somewhat seriously. "Whoever procured that skeleton may well be the answer to our riddle."

Tony typed *Nursing Schools, Chicago, 1930s* into the search bar and hit enter.

He instantly was sent down a rabbit hole of information that may or may not be what he hoped to find.

"This could take a while," he said. "Maybe I should come back later."

"That's okay. It's a beautiful day and I'm not in a rush. I'll snoop around the campus a bit. Maybe check out the art gallery."

While Tony kept searching, Megan went into the student center and bought a couple of drinks and cookies. She dropped a set off for Tony, then embarked on her stroll around the wooded college campus.

Tony discovered that there were several nursing schools in Chicago during the time period in question. One stood out. The City College of Nursing had been around since the late 1800s, but closed its doors in 1932.

That must be the college where the skeleton came from,

thought Tony.

Upon searching deeper, he discovered that the City College of Nursing didn't simply close. It was absorbed into a larger, public university, where it became their school of nursing in 1933.

The skeleton must not have been included in the merger, he thought.

Tony wanted to know more about the City College of Nursing and decided to try a different search approach. Instead of Google, he went to ebay and typed in the name of that institution and 1930s, hoping to find some memorabilia from the college.

Three screens down he found something that looked promising: a yearbook. Embossed on the leatherette cover were the words *The Nightingale, 1932, City College of Nursing.*

He clicked through the sample pages of the vintage book. Besides the cover, several inside pages were shown. They included faculty, clubs, history of the college, memorable activities and the usual head shots of individual students, each decked out in her nifty, little white cap.

When Megan returned, he was excited to tell her what he'd discovered.

"I found a yearbook from a nursing school that might be where our skeleton came from," he said. "I couldn't tell too much from the sample pages, but it seems like it might be helpful."

"Did you bid on it?"

"Better. There was a Buy it Now for only $16.99 and free shipping."

* * * * *

Tony could hardly wait to open the package that arrived three days later.

He immediately began paging through the musty yearbook, hoping that something would stand out. He scanned the names on each page, searching for anyone named Jackson.

No Jacksons.

He started over from the beginning, this time looking at the pages more broadly, occasionally reading the comments penned in the margins by classmates. The book apparently belonged to someone named Delores. Delores appeared to have had many friends, based on the number of inscriptions.

A photo spread near the center of the book was a montage of snapshots from various social events that had been held during the year. *The girls looked like they had fun,* he thought.

Tony was enjoying his journey down Delores's memory lane when something in one of the more humorous pictures caught his attention. He looked at it closely, then got the brass magnifying glass he'd found at Goodwill.

"Megan, you need to see this," he called.

"What did you find?"

"It's a picture from a Christmas party. Check out who's dressed up as Santa Claus."

He handed the glass to Megan.

"Oh my gosh! Is it... ?"

"It's got to be. Mighty skinny for Santa Claus, don't

you think?"

Megan positioned the glass over a different picture.

"Here he is again."

This time, the figure was dressed up like a dapper young dandy from the Roaring Twenties, surrounded by a group of fawning nursing students dressed like flappers."

"Did you ever wonder what went on at an all girls school?" Megan asked.

"Can't say that I did. But I wouldn't have imagined that their ideal boyfriend would be a skeleton dressed for each occasion."

"Do you suppose that's our skeleton?"

"It's got to be," Tony laughed. "He's still playing dress up!"

"Look what's written here in the margin:

Delores, what would we do without Mr. Bones to keep us company? He's almost as good a looker as George. Let's stay in touch after graduation. Love, Sophie

Megan looked at Tony, stunned.

"Look at the girl pretending to sit on Santa Bones' lap," instructed Tony. "And the girl who's holding hands with Bones Gatsby in the other picture. That's the same girl. Does she look familiar to you?"

Megan's eyes lit up. She hurried to the Victrola, grabbed the picture from their collection of clues, and handed it to Tony.

"Compare the pictures."

It took him only a moment.

"That's our Sophie!"

Tony flipped the yearbook pages ahead to the individual students' portraits. He scanned through them, looking for someone named Sophie.

"Here's the Delores who owned this book," he said, then kept paging forward.

"I found a Sophie. Sophie Jacobs."

Megan leaned in for a closer look.

"No," she said. "Wrong shaped face."

He flipped a few more pages.

"How about this one?"

He pointed to the picture beside the name Sophie Schmidt.

"That's her!" said Megan without hesitation. "Same cute, round face and sweet, innocent smile. What's it say about her?"

"She's from Rockford, Illinois."

"That's it?"

"They don't give many details. The only other thing listed for each girl is a favorite literary quotation under the name. Sophie's quote is:

> *'I had that familiar conviction that life was beginning over again with the summer.' —Jay Gatsby.*

Tony focused on her picture.

Sophie Schmidt from Rockford, Illinois, what do you want to tell us?

Chapter 32

"So," said Megan, "we now know that George Jackson and Sophie Schmidt were an item the same year that George died. I wonder what happened to Sophie?"

"We should give Jackson a call and see if he learned anything more about George's death," said Tony. "If he did, maybe he also came across something relating to Sophie."

"It's worth a try. We never did get back to him about the whiskey."

"The whiskey can wait. The longer it ages the better, right?"

Megan picked up her phone and called the last number she had for Jackson.

Much to her surprise, he answered.

She explained what they'd discovered and asked him if he'd run across anything new about George.

"No one seems to know much about him," Jackson said. "Seems like he simply vanished from the family history. Of course, anyone who knew him personally is long dead, too."

"Did you happen to find anything relating to a Sophie Schmidt?"

"No. But, then, I wasn't looking for info about anyone by that name. Let me search a little deeper. I know a guy at the Vital Records Department. Maybe he can tell me exactly when George died and how. I'll request info about Sophie Schmidt, too. Where did you say she was from?"

"Her yearbook says her hometown was Rockford."

"Okay. That's good to know. I'm planning to come back up there in a couple of days and I'll stop by with a report when I return. Enjoy the beautiful weather."

* * * * * *

Megan and Tony were sitting in their lawn chairs watching the heron catch a fish when they heard a vehicle coming up their road.

"Jackson must be back," said Tony. "I wonder what he discovered."

Instead of Jackson's camper pulling into their clearing, the vehicle that drove up to Blackbird Cabin was a police car.

"That can't be good," said Tony.

"Maybe they found out something about the skeleton in the lake."

The officer met Tony and Megan in front of the cabin.

"Hello, what can we do for you?" Tony said.

"Do you know a Fred Jackson?" the officer asked.

"We do," said Megan. "Why?"

"He was in a traffic accident."

"Is he okay?" Megan asked.

"He's been taken to the hospital in Wausau. He's pretty

banged up, but he'll be okay."

"What happened?" asked Tony.

"It appears that he was run off the road. The other vehicle fled the scene without stopping."

"That's terrible," said Megan. "Why are you contacting us?"

"He requested that we get in touch with you. His phone was damaged and he didn't have your number written down, so that's why I'm here in person. The hospital will only discharge him to a responsible person who can stay with him for the first twenty-four hours. Plus, he said he has something important to tell you."

* * * * *

They arrived at the hospital about an hour later. Jackson was sitting in a wheelchair, his arm in a sling. His face was bruised and decorated with a half dozen steri-strips. Seeing him looking so sad lowered the couple's level of annoyance for being summoned to pick him up.

"You look like you've been hit by a truck," joked Tony, trying not to sound upset.

"Almost," said Jackson. "It was dark so all I saw were headlights suddenly coming right at me. I hit the ditch. The camper tipped and slid into a tree on its side."

"We're glad you survived," said Megan. "You can stay in our guest room tonight so we can watch you. Hospital rules. Then, where should we take you?"

"If we can stop at Walmart to pick up a cot and pillow, I'll be fine in my garage until I get my new camper. I've had my eye on one for a while, so I guess now's the time to get it. Doubt I'll have much trade-in value, though."

An orderly rolled him out of the hospital and Tony helped him into their car.

"I really appreciate your doing this," Jackson said as they pulled out of the parking lot. "I didn't know who else to call. Which reminds me: I need to add 'new phone' to the Walmart list. I guess I'll need a couple sets of clothes, too, until I'm able to retrieve my own from the camper."

Jackson leaned back and closed his eyes. It was obvious that he was tired and hurting. Megan and Tony drove on in silence to allow him to rest.

Jackson was pretty dopey from the pain medication the hospital had given him, so they waited until the next morning to ask what it was he wanted to tell them.

"The officer said you had something to tell us," Megan said as they ate breakfast.

"Right," said Jackson. "My guy at vital records was able to locate the birth and death records for George. As I told you, his head stone has that he died in 1932. That's only partially true. That was the year he disappeared. He was officially declared dead seven years later, after the required waiting time for when a body is not found."

"So the skeleton I found in the lake could be George?" speculated Tony,

"Looks that way. You didn't find a second skeleton, did you?"

"No. Why?"

"Sophie Schmidt went missing the same time as George."

"Let me get this straight," said Tony, letting the new

information sink in. "George went missing in 1932. His body was never found and he was officially declared dead seven years later."

"Correct," said Jackson.

"Which means it is possible that he is the skeleton in our lake."

"Two for two."

"Sophie, George's girlfriend, went missing at the same time as George and, like George, she has never been found."

"Yes."

"What about George's grave in Chicago?" asked Megan. "Who is buried there?"

"I'm guessing it's a decoy," speculated Jackson. "Someone put up a stone for George to keep people from realizing his body was disposed of up here in the Northwoods. When we talked on the phone last week, I mentioned that there was something about the head stone that seemed off. I went back and measured the grave sites in the family plot. George's grave seems to be only two feet wide. That's not enough room for a casket. It's stuck in between a couple of other, even older graves."

"Maybe he was cremated," offered Megan. "It doesn't take much space to bury an urn."

"Cremation wasn't very common back then," said Tony.

"It definitely wouldn't have been considered in our pious Catholic family," said Jackson. "The Jacksons had proper funerals and burials, like God intended."

"So who placed George's head stone over a nonexistent grave?" asked Tony. "Aren't there rules about that? You can't just pick up a headstone at Dollar Tree."

"Remember our visit to that antique store?" said Megan. "We found a bunch of sample headstones there."

"That's true," added Tony. "They were all different sizes and unusual colors."

"Which would explain why George's stone doesn't match the others in the plot," said Jackson. "They just needed to find someone who could chisel in the name and dates."

Tony took a deep breath and exhaled slowly.

"We now have come up with three possibilities for who the skeleton in the lake could be:

"One: It's the bank robber. That was our first guess. He stumbled upon the cabin while he was evading the police and was killed by George, who kept the cash and threw the body in the lake."

"Or," interjected Megan, "maybe the robber was George."

"Don't get ahead of me."

"Two: The body in the lake is George. Maybe the robber killed him, but maybe nobody killed him. Since this was his cabin, he could have simply fallen in the lake and drowned. There were no obvious signs of violence on the skeleton."

"I'll bet he had some help falling in the lake," Jackson speculated.

"Three: The skeleton is the bogus police inspector who was killed by bootleggers in the Holy Land and then brought up here and hidden."

"That makes sense," said Jackson. "I can easily imagine that bootleggers would work together to get rid of the cops who were shaking them down."

"I still think that it's George," Megan said. "Mr. Bones in the spring house is dressed like George, which seems to be pointing to him being the skeleton in the lake."

Megan made a guess as if she were playing Clue.

"I believe it's Mr. Bones... in the spring house... with the knife. Can anyone disprove my theory?"

Tony made believe he was showing Megan a card from the Clue deck.

"I can disprove that Mr. Bones was the killer," he laughed. "Mr. Bones is a skeleton, dressed like George, with a knife in his chest. He can't be the killer because he's the victim."

"Which is my point. Mr. Bones is showing us that George is the victim."

"Which brings up an important question," said Jackson. "Who dressed up Mr. Bones as George? That person must be his killer."

"That's it!" proclaimed Megan. "Based on the yearbook pictures, the dresser would have to be Sophie. Sophie killed George! "

"Why?"

"Maybe it was a lover's quarrel."

"Then what happened to Sophie?"

"She pulled a Romeo and Juliet and killed herself."

"Try this on for size," said Jackson. "Grandpa Zee found out that Sophie had killed his brother and, to get revenge, he had one of his low-life buddies take her out. Hell, maybe he even killed her himself."

"You're not a big fan of your grandpa, are you?"

"That obvious?"

Tony broke the suddenly awkward silence.

"This was a fun exercise," he said, "but what's our next step?"

"For me," said Jackson, "the next step better be getting myself a place to live."

* * * * * *

Tony and Megan spent the next day helping Jackson get his life back in order. His camper had been towed to the local RV dealer, so he was able to retrieve his belongings. The dealership offered him a couple thousand dollars trade in toward the camper he'd had his eye on, so he decided to make the deal on the spot.

While he was filling out the paperwork, Tony and Megan went across the road to pick up some snacks and supplies at the home improvement store. When they came out, Tony was proudly waiting for them in his new camper.

"I'd like to take you out for supper," he said. "How about we try the supper club on the old highway? It's a ways out of town, but the food is excellent. Consider it my thank you for rescuing me from the hospital."

"Sounds good," said Tony. "One condition. We talk about something other than skeletons."

Chapter 33

The sun was getting low when Megan and Tony returned to Blackbird Cabin. It had been an interesting and fun day. They were glad to have helped Jackson get resettled and appreciated his taking them out for supper. It'd been a while since they'd gone out to eat somewhere fancier than the Pizza Hideaway. It was a long drive, but on such a beautiful day, it had been an enjoyable change of scenery.

Megan breathed in the pine scented air and thought to herself how lucky they were to have found their retirement cabin on the lake, just like they'd dreamed about.

She put the key in the lock. Without her turning it, the door popped open.

"We left in such a hurry this morning," she commented, "we forgot to lock the door."

She stepped inside the unlit cabin and screamed.

Someone was relaxing in the chair in front of the fireplace, a bottle of Old Blackbird Whiskey in his hand.

Megan flipped on the light. It was Mr. Bones. The knife was still stuck in his chest holding the note.

"What the hell!" said Tony, hurrying in behind her. "How did... ?"

Tony quickly checked the other rooms in the cabin. No one was in there with them. Nothing else seemed to be disturbed.

"Who would do this?" said Megan, staring at the skeleton.

"We know it wasn't Jackson. We were with him all day."

Megan focused on the note. Something was different about it. She flattened the sheet without removing it. It was the same yellowed piece of paper that had been stuck in the skeleton's chest in the spring house, but the original message was now facing down, against the body. The writing on the side facing them hadn't been there before.

"Look at this," she said.

You'll get what's coming to you!

Beneath the handwritten message was a familiar-looking *Z*.

This time, however, the mark of *Z* had something extra. Drawn over the letter were three vertical lines, almost mimicking a dollar sign, with a Z instead of an S.

"We need to check out the spring house," said Tony. "Grab the lanterns. I'll bring the grub hoe."

"Grub hoe?"

"It's the closest thing I've got to a weapon."

"If you think we need a weapon, we're not going in there."

"Let's at least go to the barn and see how things look."

They could tell by the bent-over grass that a vehicle had driven up to the barn door. Whoever visited them seemed to have known where they were going.

The barn door was still open.

Tony switched on his lantern and shined it inside. The room appeared to be empty.

They stood still for a minute, listening. The only sound was the faraway trickling of the spring.

Tony slowly walked toward the hidden entrance to the spring house, shining his light all around the inside of the barn. Aside from the blackbird cabinet door being open, everything looked the same.

"It looks safe. I'm going inside."

"Wait for me."

Megan hurried into the barn behind him, providing additional light. She followed Tony through the second door into the dank spring house. They could see scuffing on the floor. No, it wasn't scuffing, it was wheel tracks.

Everything else was as they remembered until they got about halfway to the spring. The shelves where the full bottles of whiskey had been hidden were empty. The cases with the empty bottles were piled on the floor. The full cases had been removed.

"Who knew about the whiskey?" said Megan.

"The only person we've told was Jackson."

"And he told his cousin."

"That bastard! He took us out to eat so we wouldn't be here and his cousin could come in and steal the whiskey. I knew we shouldn't trust him."

"What about your woulda, coulda, shoulda rule?"

"I woulda like to tell Mr. Jackson where he coulda stick his stupid meal. Do we know where his garage is?"

"All I know is it's somewhere in the area on a lake."

"That narrows it down to about half the places in the county."

Megan made her way to the end of the spring house and studied the spot where Mr. Bones had been sitting on a wooden crate. The crate was still there. Based on the amount of undisturbed dirt on the floor around the trunk, it hadn't been moved in a long, long time.

The wooden box the skeleton had been sitting on was sturdy and had a lid. There was a rope handle on each side. The lid was latched at the back with hinges. A rusty padlock hung from a clasp on the front.

"Tony, come and take a look at this trunk."

Tony's additional light allowed them to see that there were letters stenciled on the side. Most of the paint had flaked off in the damp environment, but it was still possible to read: PROPERTY OF Z. JACKSON.

Tony grabbed one of the handles and gave it a gentle tug. It was heavy and barely moved.

"Should we open it?" Megan asked.

Tony pulled on the lock, but it stayed closed.

"Lets take it out of here where we can better see what we're doing."

They half carried, half dragged the trunk down the slick wooden walkway, through the hidden door and into the barn.

"Wow, that thing feels like it's filled with rocks," Megan said.

Tony picked up the grub hoe and whacked it against the lock. It didn't open, but the clasp was so rusty that it pulled right off the wooden chest.

"Ready?" said Tony, grabbing the lid with two hands.

Megan positioned the lanterns so they'd provide the best illumination of the box's contents.

The lid creaked open on its rusty hinges.

It was a tool box. Clipped onto the inside of the lid were a couple of saws and a small square, each secured in its own spot. A tray filled with screw drivers, pliers, wrenches and various other hand tools filled the top third of the box. There was a handle in the center of the tray so it could be raised up to get to the contents below.

"I can save some of these tools," Tony said. "They used to make them a lot better than the tools today. They should clean up fine.

Tony lifted the tray, expecting to find heavier tools in the lower compartment, such as hammers, files and pipe wrenches.

Instead, all he saw were pieces of cloth.

"Looks like someone's old painting rags," said Megan, noticing the stains on them. "Hardly seems worth saving."

Maybe there are some more tools under the rags."

He used a screwdriver to pull out the disgusting looking fabric and tossed it onto the floor. The only things beneath it were a few old screws and bolts and a rust encrusted chisel.

Megan noticed something about the rags. There were buttons attached to them. She spread them out with her foot.

"Tony," she said. "These aren't rags. They're clothes."

She knelt down and gently spread out the garments. A blouse and a skirt. Not very large. Something a young woman might have worn in the 1930s.

"Looks like we can rule out Sophie as George's killer," said Megan as she stared at the clothing.

"Her body is probably hidden somewhere around here," said Tony. "Maybe in the woods. I suppose we need to contact the sheriff again."

"And tell them what? That someone took our bootleg whiskey, which may or may not be legal for us to have? That there's an uninvited skeleton enjoying a stiff drink in our living room? A skeleton that we conveniently didn't tell them about the last time they were here. That we discovered some old clothes in a tool box, that might be nothing more than shop rags but could be the clothes worn by a young woman who was murdered here? They'll race right over and haul us to the looney bin."

"Point taken," said Tony. "I don't want to make that call, either."

"The first thing we need to do is get ahold of Jackson and hear his explanation for the whiskey being taken."

"Can you give him a call?"

"I left my phone in the cabin. Not sure that'll do any good, anyway. Who knows if he's got the same number on his new phone."

"Only one way to find out. I think we're done in here for now. Let's leave everything right where it is. Tomorrow, when there's better light, I'd like to take some pictures of the 'crime scenes.'"

"We've still got the crime scene tape they took down after they were finished at the dam," snarked Megan. "I could put that up for you and make your pictures look really official. Maybe I could even make you some cute little sandwich boards with numbers on them."

"I don't think you're taking this seriously," said Tony.

"I am, actually," she said as they reached the cabin

door. "But I am also exhausted and need to forget about this skeleton thing for awhile."

"Good luck with that," Tony said as they stepped into the cabin and were greeted by Mr. Bones. "I hope he's willing to share his drink."

Chapter 34

They hadn't been able to reach Jackson the previous night, but before they tried calling him again the next morning, his camper pulled up to Blackbird Cabin.

"We've got a question for you," Tony demanded.

"I'm sure you do," he said, getting out of the camper and holding up his hands in innocence. "It was my cousin. When I got back last night, he was parked in my driveway and told me he'd picked up the whiskey and assured me he would settle up with us once he's sold it."

"But we hadn't agreed to anything," said Megan. "Why would he just assume he could come by and take what wasn't his?"

"Well, I guess he kinda made that assumption based on me telling him that I was sure you'd be fine with the agreement."

"That was pretty rotten. Did he tell you about the skeleton?"

"He did," Jackson laughed. "He said he wanted to make sure you wouldn't miss the note explaining that he'd been here and let you know you'd get your share. For a guy who's kind of an A-hole, he's got a good sense of humor."

"He's also got a weird concept of explaining," said

Tony. "The note said, *You'll get what's coming to you!* That sounds more like a threat than an explanation."

"And signing it with the letter Z only made it feel more threatening," added Megan. She went inside and brought out the note. "Look at this."

"That's pretty cool," said Jackson. "I've never really seen his word mark before. Very clever."

"Clever?"

"Sure. He's Zachary Jackson the third. Get it? The letter Z and the Roman numeral for three. Kinda looks like a dollar sign, which is perfect for a guy who loves money."

"Are all you Jacksons this weird?" questioned Megan.

"We do our best."

"We're none too happy about your cousin raiding our whiskey stash," said Tony, "but because of him moving Mr. Bones, we think we now know what happened to Sophie. You need to see something we found in the spring house."

The sun was shining through the open barn door and windows, giving the group a clear view of the items spread out on the floor.

"The skeleton was sitting on this tool chest," said Megan. "We decided to see what was inside and found these."

She motioned with her toe to the skirt and blouse that were spread out on the floor.

"I checked the photo we found in the lamp and these look like the clothes Sophie was wearing in the picture with George."

"And the skeleton was wearing George's clothes," added Tony. "We believe someone killed them both."

"It does look that way, doesn't it," said Jackson. "I'll bet it was the bank robber. He killed them, then fled in a panic, leaving the money behind, afraid to come back for it."

"We don't think so," said Megan. "Look at this."

She pointed out the faint words stenciled onto the side of the tool box: PROPERTY OF Z. JACKSON.

"Sophie's clothes were hidden in the bottom of your grandpa's tool box," she said. "It would appear that your grandfather killed his brother George and George's girlfriend, Sophie, and hid their bodies here."

"Have you found Sophie?"

"No, but it's a big woods," said Tony.

"After this much time," Megan added, "I doubt that even the best cadaver dog could find her remains, if they even still exist."

"And," continued Tony, "I'm sure the authorities would have little interest in spending either the time or the resources needed for the search."

"Not to mention," said Jackson, "they'd never agree on whose jurisdiction it was. It would depend on if they were killed here in the Northwoods or in Chicago."

The trio walked silently back to the cabin.

Jackson broke the silence.

"I'm glad that Grandpa is dead. I'd hate to see a hundred-year-old man being tried for a double homicide. He went to his grave sure that he'd pulled off the perfect crime."

"I'm sure St. Peter gave him a hero's welcome at the pearly gates," said Megan sarcastically.

Chapter 35

Megan, Tony and Jackson decided to keep their latest discoveries to themselves.

They brought Sophie's skirt and blouse out to the lake and set them atop a small raft they'd built from branches that had been pulled from the old beaver dam, where George's body had been found and where some of his remains probably still existed. Solemnly and reverently they set the raft on fire and pushed it out onto the lake, silently bidding her farewell as they watched the last remnants of her existence disappear.

Then the threesome drove out to the antique store and purchased the smallest of the sample headstones. Tony used the chisel he'd found in Grandpa's tool box to add her name. It seemed both wrong and fitting that a tool that had been held in *Z*'s hands should be used to commemorate the young woman whose life he had taken.

Jackson agreed to transport Sophie's stone to the cemetery and discretely place it next to the stone commemorating George. Their memorials would be only a few yards from Grandpa Jackson's grave, where the two of them could mock his soul for all eternity.

Chapter 36

Megan and Tony enjoyed the rest of the summer at their cabin on the lake without incident. Tony completed the trail surrounding the lake and Megan extended the landscaping to the area around the new bridge. She decided that would be a lovely spot for Tony to build a little screened-in gazebo. He put it on the to-do list for the next summer.

They didn't see Jackson again and made no attempt to discover the location of his garage. Their time together was a memory they'd never forget, but they had no desire to extend.

Every so often they'd get an unsigned greeting card in the mail. It might say *Happy Birthday*, or *Congratulations* or *Have a Spooky Halloween*. Included in the envelope would be some cash, usually a combination of fifty and hundred dollar bills. The postmark was always Chicago.

When the weather cooled down, Tony began work on his ripped-from-the-headlines novel. He had never expected that some of those headlines would be of their own making.

He called the novel "The Secret of Blackbird Cabin"

and based it loosely on the experiences he and Megan had had the previous summer. The old adage that *authors should write what they know* came in handy, although he quickly recognized that there were a number of things he didn't actually know, questions that had never truly been answered. That was okay. He was a novelist, not a historian. He had the freedom to weave the story however he wanted, with whatever twists and turns he felt were appropriate to the tale he was telling.

As in all novels based on true incidents, he felt compelled to change the characters' identities.

He first created a fictional couple named Randy and Donna. The story began when they discovered a for sale notice for a rustic little cabin on a lake.

Fred Jackson became a character named Carl Thompson. He simply went by Thompson.

Thompson's grandfather, who had recently died, was Zander Thompson. Tony wasn't willing to give up that important character's word mark and had to find an old-fashioned name that started with the letter Z.

One character whose name he didn't change was Dawn Hogan from Channel 12. Tony was confident she'd be flattered to be included and he believed that including her gave the novel a sense of reality, just like screen writers often included real-life news casters in their movies to give the story a feeling of authenticity.

Dawn's well-crafted reports about the bank loot and skeleton in the lake had put her on the radar of news directors in larger markets and within a few months she'd been snapped up by a station in Nashville.

Renaming George and Sophie was difficult. Both he

and Megan felt as if they had become friends with the young couple and wanted to give them the future together they never got to enjoy. Someone needed to protect their memory.

Nevertheless, Tony decided it would be best to change their names, the same as he'd done for most of the other characters.

"I need a consult," he said to Megan. "What would you think if George became Jay? I think he kinda looks like the character in The Great Gatsby. And Sophie could be named Daisy, Gatsby's love interest."

"You do realize neither of those characters is particularly likeable, right?"

"To be honest, I don't actually remember much about the story other than how they looked."

Megan pulled out her phone and searched for the most popular baby names in the early 1900s.

"The two most popular names nearly every year in the decade George and Sophie were born was John for boys and Mary for girls."

"Boring."

"George is number five. I don't find Sophie at all."

She continued looking through the list.

"How about Geoff and Sallie?"

"That has a nice ring to it. Geoff and Sallie it is. Thank you Megan... or should I say Donna?"

"You're welcome... Randy."

Tony wrote and rewrote throughout the winter. Megan read each of his chapters as they appeared, offering her comments and suggestions. By the time the last snow had fallen, "The Secret of Blackbird Cabin" was complete.

Chapter 37

A month after "The Secret of Blackbird Cabin" was published, Tony had an author's program and book signing at the Northland Public Library. A week earlier he'd been interviewed live on Channel 12 and had been featured in the weekly shopping paper, so the public was aware of his new novel. There was a good turnout.

A young woman lingered in the library after the program. When Tony and Megan were about to leave, she stepped back into the meeting room clutching her copy of "The Secret of Blackbird Cabin" along with a worn pocket folder.

"I really enjoyed your book," she said. "Would you sign my copy?"

"I'm glad you enjoyed it," said Tony, taking a Sharpie out of his pocket. "Should I make it out to anyone in particular?"

"Make it out to Sophie."

"Nice name," he said as he signed her book and handed it back.

She smiled and said, "Your description of the picture of Geoff and Sallie sitting on the running board of their old car reminded me of a picture of my great grandmother and great grandfather, Betty and Howard. ”

Sophie opened up the pocket folder and removed an art deco cardboard frame. She held out the framed picture for Tony and Megan to see.

“This is Betty and Howard when they were young.”

Tony and Megan looked at each other, speechless.

“I found the picture along with some other papers that were my grandma’s,” Sophie continued. “It reminds me of the way you described Geoff and Sallie’s picture that was found in the oil lamp. I thought you might get a kick out of seeing it.”

Megan sat down. Tony put his hand on the back of her chair.

“Where did you get that?” Megan asked, almost under her breath.

“When Great Grandma Betty died, this folder was clipped to her will, with the instructions that it not be opened until she was gone. Her daughter, my grandma, took it, but didn’t show it to anyone else. I don’t think she even read it all the way through, herself.”

“When was that?”

“About twenty-five years ago. I ended up with it last year when my grandma died and her things were divided among the family members. It was in a cardboard box filled with old pictures and papers that no one wanted to sort through.”

“Why didn’t your grandmother want anyone to see it?”

“I don’t think it was the picture. I think she was embarrassed by a story her mother had written that was with the picture. Great Grandma suffered from dementia the last years of her life. Much of what she said had no bearing in fact."

"What was the story?" Megan asked.

"She said that her name wasn't really Betty Rivers and that her husband wasn't actually Howard Rivers. Her tale had a lot of similarities to 'The Secret of Blackbird Cabin.' The people she described in her story reminded me of Geoff and Sallie, the characters in your novel. But that's not the names she gave them in her story."

Tony also sat down. He pulled out a chair for Sophie.

"What did she say their names actually were?" he asked.

"She wrote that her name was originally Sophie Schmidt and Great Grandpa originally called himself George Jackson. She weaved a fanciful tale about how they'd gone into hiding after witnessing a murder, fled to California where they could blend in with the thousand of Oakies that were moving there at the time, and changed their names to Howard and Betty Rivers."

Tony opened his mouth to speak, then paused to gather his thoughts.

"I made up the names Geoff and Sallie for the book," he said. "Their real names were George and Sophie. George Jackson and Sophie Schmidt."

Sophie reached into her pocket folder and removed a small stack of handwritten pages held together with a paper clip.

"I think you'll want to read this," she said.

To Be Read Only After My Death

The Story of
Howard & Betty Rivers

--Betty Rivers

You know me as Betty Rivers.

That is a lie.

My actual name is Sophie Schmidt. I was born in Rockford, Illinois, not Oklahoma as I have always told you. My family did not move to California from Oklahoma looking for a better life when I was a child.

All of that was a lie.

My husband of 49 years was not Howard Rivers. His real name was George Jackson and he was from Chicago.

Maybe you've heard the heartwarming story of how Howard and I met at the county fair in Bakersfield. Once again, that was not the truth.

It was true that I fled to California, but I fled there with George. We started a new life together, in a new part of the country, with new identities.

Our families did not know where we had gone. In fact, they were led to believe, by us, that George and I were both dead.

I'm sorry that we deceived you. I am writing this in the hopes that when you know why we did what we did, you will forgive us for misleading you all these many years.

I am the last person alive who knows what really happened back then. Once I am gone, the truth will be lost forever. It is time for our story to be told.

George and I met when I was a first-year nursing student in Chicago. He delivered medicinal alcohol to the hospital and before we knew it, we were dating.

It wasn't until a year later that I learned that George and a couple of his buddies had begun a bootlegging operation in northern Wisconsin. He named his whiskey after my favorite song, Bye, Bye Blackbird. We had danced to that song the first time we went out together.

George's brother, Zachary — everyone called him Zee — was in charge of distributing the whiskey that George made. It went to the speakeasies in Chicagoland. Zee worked with a number of other bootleggers, too, but I tried to stay out of their business.

Zee was not a nice person. He repeatedly tried to lure me away from George, but I had no interest in him, which infuriated him. No one said 'no' to Zachary Jackson!

I would sometimes spend time at the cabin where the whiskey was being made. They had quite an operation in what appeared to be a barn, but was actually a cover for their still. They even had a huge cave-like structure where they could hide and age their whiskey.

One weekend while I was up north visiting George — I'd taken the train which had a stop about 20 miles from the cabin — Zee arrived to haul a shipment of Old Blackbird Whiskey back to Chicago.

George was in the spring house and I was in the cabin alone when Zee arrived. He tried to have his way with me. He called me a very bad name when I pushed him away. He tried again, more forcefully and I kneed him in the privates. He stormed out and began loading his truck.

When George came back into the cabin a few minutes later, he could tell something was wrong. I told him what had happened and he confronted his brother, who swore it was all a misunderstanding.

I could tell that George did not believe

him. As Zee drove away, George hollered to him that this was not the end of the matter and he was not welcome to set foot on the property again.

That should have been the end of it, but it wasn't. Zee had some bootlegger friends in a part of the state called the Holy Land. They had killed a guy who was shaking them down by posing as a cop, and Zee suggested they take the body to George's cabin and bury it in his woods.

George would have no part of it. He never did know where they hid the body. He was furious that Zee had sent them to his place where he could be connected to a murder.

A couple of weeks after that, Zee showed up again to get another load of whiskey. I was in Chicago, so I'm telling this second hand.

  Zee decided it was too late to head back to Chicago and decided to stay the night in the cabin. George told him he was not welcome in the cabin and he'd have to sleep in the barn.

  During the night, someone snuck inside the barn, waking Zee, who was already furious for being made to sleep in there. It was a fugitive robber who had stolen money from a bank in Michigan. He begged Zee to let him hide there until the heat was off. Zee assured him that he'd make sure no one would find him. Ever.

  George came out at sunrise the next morning and found Zee dragging a naked body down to the lake. Zee told his brother how lucky it was that this guy had literally walked in the door with thousands of dollars ready for the taking. The best part was that no one knew where this guy was.

George told him he wanted nothing to do with it. Zee just laughed and dragged the robber's body over to the beaver dam, where he pushed it to the bottom and held it down with brush and logs.

By the time Zee came back to the cabin, George had hidden the stolen money in a hidey hole he'd earlier created behind a kitchen cabinet. Only George (and later, I) knew about that secret hiding spot.

Zee was furious that George had taken the money. He pulled his gun — Zee always carried a gun, he was a part-time RR cop after all — but it was wet and wouldn't fire. He swore to George that the next time he saw him, he'd be joining the robber at the bottom of the lake. Then he added that George should not expect to see his girlfriend — me — alive again. Zee jumped into his truck and roared out of the driveway.

Soon after Zee left, George got in his car and headed straight to Chicago. He met me at the hospital, where I was working a night rotation. He looked terrified. Said that he feared for both of our lives and that we needed to hide someplace where Zee couldn't track us down.

We spent the night in George's coupe parked along Lakeshore Drive. We didn't get any sleep. By the morning, we had come up with a plan.

We'd been reading news stories about the many families and individuals that were packing their belongings into their cars and heading to California. They were called Oakies, but not all of them were from Oklahoma. They were simply hard-on-their-luck folks who had decided to start their lives over.

We definitely felt the need to start our lives over. Before we left, though, we decided to set a trap so that if Zee ever tried to come after us, the truth would be revealed, even if he had succeeded in killing us.

George snuck into Zee's house and stole his tool chest and police badge. Then he left a note for Zee telling him that he was never to set foot in the cabin again or all hell would break lose on him. He'd be linked to a variety of crimes.

I 'borrowed' Mr. Bones from the nursing school, which was going out of business anyway and wouldn't miss him.

Without telling anyone, we then drove back up to the cabin where we began setting up a series of clues that would point to Zee as being the murderer... of us. We didn't stop there. We also included clues that could incriminate him as being involved in the bank robbery and the killing of the bogus cop in the Holy Land (which we suspected might actually have been the case).

Then, as the final straw, George went to the courthouse and transferred the title to his property to Zee, which would look very suspicious in the light of our mysterious disappearance. We knew that Zee's accountant automatically paid the taxes each year for his various properties and Zee might not even notice that he was now the owner of a bootleg operation where a body was hidden.

We considered taking the loot from the bank robbery to help us get started in our new life, but decided against it. For one thing, it wasn't ours to take. We also realized that the money could probably be traced to the robbery, which would blow our new identities. And it was more satisfying to think that when the money was found, Zee would be associated with the robbery.

The final thing we did was set up the tool chest and skeleton in the spring house. If Zee did come back to see if there was any more whiskey, we wanted it to be very obvious to him that we meant business when we said we'd set up clues pointing to him as our murderer.

I felt bad spilling beef blood on my favorite blouse, the one I was wearing in the picture of George and I in his new car, but we were taking seriously our framing of Zee for our murder. We wanted to make it obvious who the clothes belonged to.

I had fun rewriting the lyrics to Bye, Bye Blackbird, which could serve as a guide to finding the clues that we'd left. Before locking up the cabin, we danced together as 'our' song played on the Victrola.

Our new life in California was marvelous. We chose the name Rivers because a river always moves forward and never looks back.

We did miss the Northwoods of Wisconsin, though, and did return as tourists a few times when we were older, but we never did go back to the cabin. We were thrilled when our grandson decided to take a job Up North.

After George died, I moved back to Wisconsin, to an assisted living apartment, fittingly along a river, not many miles from the cabin. I'm writing this story as I sit on my balcony watching the water flow by, always moving forward.

A few months ago, my first great grand-child was born. A little girl. When her parents were considering baby names, I had mentioned to them that the name Sophie was always special to me. I was thrilled when that was the name they'd chosen.

My dear, sweet Sophie, if you are reading this, you'll now know why I hug you so tightly. And why I sometimes call you my little Blackbird.

—Betty Rivers (AKA Sophie Jackson)